Forgotten Magic

Forgotten Magic

Sandra Rose Wild

To order additional copies of this book, contact:
Xlibris
800-056-3182
www.Xlibrispublishing.co.uk
Orders@Xlibrispublishing.co.uk
710685

CONTENTS

For my husband John; my sons Charles and John; to the cherished memory of my daughter Suzanne, and with thanks to my family together with all the friends who have journeyed with me through this magical tale.

THE WATCHER IN THE DARK

James Cadwallader stood in the doorway of his sister's bedroom and smiled as he watched her. She looked so peaceful as she slept, her cheeks all flushed and rosy like two bright, shiny apples. He wondered what she was dreaming about. Her birthday party probably, when in a few days time, she would be five. She was cheeky and bright, and he felt very protective towards her, the eight-year age gap between them making no difference to their companionship. He was her big brother, and even when he tried to avoid her, she would find him, wanting to join in, scribbling on his homework and tormenting his friends. Her name was Daisy, after their great-grandmother. She had the same wavy, golden hair, cornflower-blue eyes, and affectionate personality. Earlier, he'd knocked on the door of his father's study, wanting to wish him good night, but there was no reply. His father was ill, but James didn't understand what was wrong with him. The dad he knew and loved was becoming a stranger, and he was beginning to worry. Sometimes he thought that he must have done something to upset him but didn't know what. He just wished his dad would get better and be his old self again.

A sudden noise caught his attention, a sharp scraping like stone against glass. The hairs on the back of his neck stood on end as he peered into the dimly lit corners of his sister's bedroom; he saw nothing. The sinister form, which watched him from behind his sister's bed, withdrew its jagged claws from beneath her pillows and crouched in the darkness. It could wait. The boy would give up his secret. He would have no choice if he wanted to save his sister, then the ancient magic would be theirs again. It would not be long before it would taste its reward. The thought of the child's warm, sweet blood was almost too much to bear as, with a sound like the ticking of cockroaches escaping from light, it drew its twisted body deeper into the gloom beneath the bed. James shivered. For a brief moment he felt strange and distant, as if someone else were in his mind. Daisy sighed in her sleep. Everything was fine. He pulled the duvet up over her shoulders before continuing on the way to his bedroom.

THE HOUSE OF WIZARDS

Deep in the woods, the inhabitants of another, very different house, were also sleeping. This was a house of mystery and magic, a house which breathed with a will of its own. All was calm and still, even the fire which burned in the great stone hearth, was silent. Nothing stirred in the massive kitchen of this ancient abode of wizards.

Mr Witty, the youngest of them and new to the house, was sprawled in an overstuffed armchair in front of the fire. His hat, which was pulled down over his eyes, was made of a soft felt, and more like a trilby in shape and size than the ones usually worn by wizards. It was olive green and had a wide, red velvet band around it, in which he wore two glossy jackdaw's feathers. His right arm dangled down over the side of the chair, just above the head of Thomas, the cat. Every couple of minutes, his fingers jerked, flicking the cat's ears. Thomas growled deep in his throat, his whiskers bristling in exasperation. He bared his claws and raised a paw to swat the wizard's hand away, just managing to stop at the very last moment before moving out of reach.

The wizard's feet rested on a table, the tips of his pointed black slippers—slippers even blacker than the cat—just visible amongst the clutter of cups, plates, paint, papers, boxes, and jars that littered its surface. His mouth was open, and he was snoring loudly. His jaws moved as if he were chewing a very sticky toffee, and his plump, whiskerless face glowed pink in the firelight.

From out of the shadows beyond the hearth, a dragon who was not much bigger than a hamster, shook his drowsy head and peered at the wizard through pale, blue eyes.

One more try, he thought. *While he's asleep.*

He leaned back on his tiny, smoke grey tail, clenched his claws together as hard as he could, squeezed his eyes tightly shut, took a deep breath, held it, and . . . *pop*! He looked around him and sighed. Nothing had happened. He just couldn't make himself invisible, no matter how hard he tried. All he ever managed was to make popping noises. He tried again, concentrating even harder. This time the *pop* was so loud that he fell over then quickly hid in the corner as Mr Witty awoke with a shout, his arms flailing as he struggled to get out of the chair. The dragon watched as the wizard's feet kicked against the tallest jar, which fell, as if in slow motion, onto the stone flagged floor, where it smashed into thousands of pieces.

Thomas was shaking his head. 'What now? Can't get a minute's peace around here!'

He arched his back as he wondered whether to find somewhere else to sleep, before glaring at the little dragon, who was about to attempt to make himself invisible yet again.

'Stop that! Now look what you've done. He's bad enough without you making him jump.'

The dragon hung his head. 'It'th not my fault. He thaid I had to practith or there'd be trouble.'

'Well, you're in big trouble now. We all are. Look!'

Smoke, the colour of custard, was pouring from the broken jar, together with the eruption of multicoloured balls of light and crackling, fiery sparks. Fizzing spells, especially designed to be a nuisance, whizzed and swooped around Mr Witty's head, whooping and shrieking like fireworks on bonfire night.

'Here's fire and smoke, |

To char and choke, |

We'll rip and rap, |

Then singe the cat,' screamed the spells before bursting into an explosion of orange fire.

Thomas howled and jumped back, his fur standing on end, as one of them flew past his nose, choking him with its sulphurous fumes.

Try as he might, the wizard's efforts to catch them in what looked like a child's fishing net was having no effect. As fast as he caught them, more appeared and he was becoming extremely annoyed.

High in the rafters, Cranlow the owl, snoozing with his head tucked under his wing, almost fell off his perch as one of the spells, sparking and spinning like a Catherine wheel, erupted behind him.

'The book!' bellowed the wizard, waving the net in the owl's direction. 'Find the book!'

Cranlow ruffled his feathers, stared at Mr Witty in disgust, and muttered, 'Hmph! Trust him not to know where it is. Any wizard worth his staff can find anything in less time than it takes a bee to buzz, but not him. And what sort of a name is that for any self-respecting wizard? Witty indeed. Now Twitty—that would suit him far better. Oh, why did I say I'd take this job? That's what you get for doing favours for friends. Well, not friends exactly—you can't really say that you can make a friend of a tree, even if it is royal and very old.'

'Now Cranlow! Get a move on before any of them manage to escape. If, it's not too much trouble for you!'

'All right! I'm going!' The owl launched himself into flight. 'Oh yes, I'm going. Just you watch me. I'm not risking my feathers for you any more. You'll miss me when I'm gone. That's if you'd even notice my extremely noticeable absence.'

Mr Witty's hat was now on fire, and he plunged it into the sink to put out the flames before turning his attention to the cat.

'Well? Don't just sit there. Help Cranlow!'

But Thomas had other ideas as, starting with his tail, he slowly disappeared, his great, green eyes gleaming with fury, winking out as suddenly as a light turned off at bedtime.

The wizard's gaze now fell upon the fearful dragon, who was driving himself into one last desperate effort to make himself invisible. He concentrated with every ounce of his being, which wasn't very much for one so small. This time, the popping noise seemed to go on forever as he felt himself falling, spinning, and tumbling helplessly through cold, dark, empty space.

WISP

'Well now. What ever is this? Looks like some sort of worm. Never seen one with wings before, besides which worms are pink, squishy things—this is a sort of dull, greyish . . .'

The little dragon opened his eyes and peered cautiously in the direction of the squeaky voice, nervously shuffling his feet. He'd landed in a narrow corridor. Thick cobwebs covered the walls and hung from the ceiling like dirty net curtains, almost reaching the floor. He sneezed as a piece of one dropped onto his face. It was sticky and cold. He sneezed again as he tried to shake it off.

'If you keep doing that, those spiders'll make a parcel out of you and hang you up in their larder.'

A tear ran down the dragon's face and then another, quickly dissolving the sticky web.

'It's crying,' said the squeaky voice again.

'Better get it out of here and have a proper look,' said an even squeakier voice.

'Well, come on then, before those spiders get you. I've heard they're quite partial to a nice worm for their supper.'

The two creatures led him down the long, dusty corridor until finally pulling him through a hole in a wall into a musty-smelling room. Great stacks of papers tottered in every corner. Some had fallen, whilst others looked as if they were about to, and some were floating high in the air as if trying to find the place to which they belonged.

'Hm. So what kind of a whatsit are you then?' asked the plumper of the two squeaks.

'I'm a dragon,' he whispered.

'A dragon!' they cried as one.

He nodded as they stared at him in astonishment.

'Name?' they asked together.

'Withp,' he breathed.

'Withp? What thort—we mean—what sort of a name is that? Don't you mean Wisp?' They couldn't hide their hilarity and had started to giggle. 'A dragon with a lisp. Who ever heard of a lithping dragon? Oh, this is too much.'

By now, the dragon's tears were making a pool on the floor.

'Please don't cry. It's not that bad. We'll be your friends. Never had a dragon for a friend before. I'm Robbit, and this here's Pest.' They both bowed.

'Oh,' said Wisp. 'Thith ith the firtht time I've ever theen a rabbit.'

'Robbit! Not *rabbit*!' They were shaking their heads. 'Are we all fluffy with big floppy ears and little stumpy tails? I don't think so. What are we indeed? We're mice of course. You know—of the cheese-eating kind? Boy! Where have you been all your life?'

'I don't really know how I got to be here with you,' said Wisp. 'That withard thaid I had to practith making mythelf invithible, and thith ith where I ended up. My parentth thent me to thith houthe. They thay I've got thom thort of thpecial magic and I'm thupothed to be helping, but I can't do anything without cauthing trouble. I can't get anything right, and now all thothe thpellth are thetting fire to Mr Witty'th hat.'

'Oh. What a sight.'

The mice were now laughing so much they had fallen flat on their backs, bare, pink feet waving as they rolled on the floor.

Wisp had begun to laugh with them before his eyes filled with tears yet again.

'What's the matter now?' they asked.

'I'm thcared,' he said eventually. I think they've all made a big mithtake. I can't do magic. I know I haven't got any and I won't ever be able to go home. My family will never thpeak to me again. I'm jutht a hopeleth failure.'

'Well. You must have done something right,' said Robbit. 'If you didn't have any magic, you'd still be in there chasing spells, wouldn't you?'

'Magic's weird,' said Pest. 'Not that I know anything, but perhaps you're trying too hard. Maybe you have to sort of—well, just let it happen.'

'Will you help me?' Wisp asked.

'Us? Help with magic? Goodness, no!'

They were both talking together again.

'But don't be upset. We'll look after you. You're in safe hands with us.'

Suddenly, the mice began to panic, looking for somewhere to hide.

'Whatever ith the matter?'

'Hush. Something's coming.'

'I can't hear anything,' Wisp whispered as they pulled him behind one of the tottering piles.

Pest's teeth were chattering with fear. Robbit put his paw over his friend's mouth and indicated to Wisp to be as quiet as possible. A shadow fell across them, and as it lengthened, all the floating papers began to gather themselves together. As they did so, the tottering stacks joined them, slowly forming into a great book which floated in the middle of the room. Their hiding place was soon gone and the mice were shaking with fright.

'Well. Well. What have we here? ' The voice was a bit hooty and rather posh.

Wisp looked up and saw Cranlow peering down at them as he hovered over the book.

'Hallo, Mr Cranlow, thir.'

The owl stared more closely at the little dragon.

'Ah,' he said. 'So this is where you ended up. I'm glad I've found you so easily. It seems Mr Twitty may need your assistance, so you'll have to come back with me. I don't like the idea either, but we aren't the ones who make the decisions around here. We just have to do as we're told, whether we like it or not.'

'Well, I don't know why he'd need me . . . and what about my friendth here?' asked Wisp, pointing to the two cowering mice

'Owls eat mice. Didn't you even know that?' whispered Robbit as he looked up at Cranlow. 'Please make it quick, Mr Owl. Please don't make us suffer.'

'Eat you?' Cranlow hooted. 'Eat you? Never! You're house mice. Far too fat and tasteless. If I ate you, I'd have indigestion for a week.'

'Really? You're not going to eat us? Oh, thank you, thank you, sir, Mr Owl, sir.'

'Yes. Yes. Well, I am very particular, you know. Now come along, hop on board, and we'll get back to that useless wizard immediately.'

Cranlow uttered some strange-sounding words, and the book slowly descended to the floor.

'Hold on tightly,' he said as they started on their way. 'I'll drop you lot off first before I deliver this to him.'

LOSING DAISY

It was breakfast time at the Cadwalladers'. James still hadn't seen his father.

'Where's Dad?' His mother was busy making toast.

'He'll be down later,' she replied as she reached for the marmalade.

'When?'

'I don't know, James. When he's ready, I suppose.'

Daisy had slopped milk and orange juice onto the table and was dabbling her hands in it. She was laughing.

'It's not funny,' James said as he mopped juice from his trousers.

'Is,' she said, about to flick cornflakes at him.

'No, Daisy! Don't you dare do that! Mum. Stop her. Please, Mum.'

But by now, his mother was busy on the telephone. Wet cornflakes landed on his arm. He picked them off and threw them back at his sister, who ducked, and they landed on her head. She frowned at him as she tried to get them out of her hair and then screamed before bursting into tears. James couldn't help grinning as he went over to her.

'It's all right, Dais. Don't cry. I'll get them.'

'No!' she shouted and screamed again.

'I'll give you sweets,' he said. 'Those nice jelly ones.'

He had to try really hard not to laugh as he looked at her. What a mess she was in with breakfast and tears smeared all over her pretty face, as well as the cornflakes in her hair. He felt guilty and gave her a hug.

'And chocolate ones as well, and play with me,' she said in a deliberately small voice through lips pushed forward into a rosebud pout.

11

'Well. I have got homework to do,' he said, trying to avoid the issue. Jelly sweets and chocolates he could manage, but playing was another matter entirely. He turned to his mother for help.

'I'm sure you'll think of something,' she said. 'And it'll serve you right for retaliating.'

'What about a nice walk?' he asked. 'Find that big pond in the woods?'

Daisy nodded. 'But I have to bring my friend too.'

'What friend?' asked James, looking at his mother. 'I don't think I can cope with more than one.'

His mother smiled. 'Don't worry, James. It's her imaginary friend, not a real one. You used to have one too, don't you remember? You never did tell us his name, but you used to talk to him all the time.'

James felt himself blushing as he said, 'I don't think I want to hear any more about that.'

He turned to his sister and asked, 'Is that who you've been talking to, Daisy?'

She nodded, looking very serious.

'What's this friend like then?'

'Well,' said Daisy. 'He's a little man, with funny hair and he's got a red hat and he can do dancing.'

'Is he some sort of elf then, like the ones in your storybook?'

'No,' she said, shaking her head. 'He's not an elf, you silly. He's a fairy man, 'cause that's what he said.'

But as she spoke, *something* was beginning to trouble James.

'What sorts of things do you talk to him about?' he asked.

'Oh, lots of things, but mostly he wants me to say things about you. I like fairies,' she said as she followed her mother out of the kitchen. 'Do you like fairies, James?'

'Oh yes,' he replied. 'I'm sure they're very nice.' But he was filled with a strange disquiet. It was like trying to remember the answer to a question. You're sure you know what it is but no matter how hard you try, it just won't come into your mind. Like his imaginary friend. He had no idea what his mother had been talking about.

He leaned on the windowsill and looked out into the garden. The house bordered woodland and was called Oakfield after the trees that stood next to it. James liked walking in the woods. There were old stories about strange happenings and one in particular about a mysterious old house, which was never to be found in the same place. Some of his friends said they'd seen it. They could never find it a second time though.

Daisy was clean and ready to go. James took her hand. 'I've got a jam jar so we can look for some tadpoles like last time, and see if the frogs are still there.'

She held his hand tightly as she clumped along the path beside him in her shocking-pink wellies, humming snatches of her favourite nursery rhymes and stamping in all the puddles.

It was quiet in the woods. Daisy had found some bluebells growing next to the pond and was busily picking them as she talked, non stop, to the battered old teddy she carried in her bag. She seemed to be more interested in them than catching any tadpoles. Every now and then she'd turn around and stop, as if listening for something.

'Can we go that way?' she asked suddenly, pointing into the trees.

'I don't think so,' James replied. 'There's no path and there are brambles everywhere.'

But she was already on her way.

'No!' He yelled. 'Come back!'

He could hear her voice. It sounded as if she were talking to someone, and it wasn't her teddy.

'Daisy!' he shouted again at the top of his voice. She didn't answer. Ivy and dead branches tripped him as he tried to follow her. Brambles caught at his jumper and wrapped around his legs as if trying to trap him, their sharp thorns cutting his hands as he pushed his way through. There was no sign of her, and he was becoming very alarmed. She couldn't have got very far, so why couldn't he find her? Something was wrong. He struggled on, calling her name. There was no reply. After what felt like hours, he came into a clearing. He was exhausted, lost, and beginning to lose his nerve.

Something brushed against his leg. He jumped and looked down. It was a cat. A very big, black cat. It stared up at him before making its way along a path that led out of the clearing. A path that James was certain hadn't been there earlier. The cat stopped and glanced back at him. The only part of it now visible, were its eyes. Two emerald green lights which seemed to float in mid-air as they blinked on and off, one after the other. He had no choice but to follow it. Strangely, the path was clear and easy to walk. He stopped, looking back the way they'd come. The path disappeared as he watched and eerie shapes slid through the undergrowth towards him. The cat wound itself around his ankles before running in front of him, urging him forward. A faint light glowed in the distance. The path appeared to be leading them towards it. As they approached, the glow became brighter, revealing a small, stone built cottage. The front door was open. A woman and child stood in the doorway. The child was Daisy.

MEETING THE MASTER

Mr Witty stood in the centre of the room, a foot tapping his impatience at being kept waiting. They all watched as Cranlow flew the Book towards him, hovering high above the kitchen table before letting it drop and land with a crash. Objects scattered in all directions. Then, as if this wasn't enough, Cranlow landed on the book and stared at the now furious wizard.

'Not had much success at cleaning up I see. I have to say I'm not surprised. 'Didn't get all those fizzers either. Look out! Here's one coming now!'

The incoming spell skimmed across the top of Mr Witty's hat causing the bedraggled jackdaw's feathers to burn momentarily, before subsiding into a thin, white smoke, which smelled like burnt cabbage.

'Oh, what a state to be in.' Cranlow was as near to crowing as an owl could get. 'Just look at you. I must say, you really are an absolute fright!'

'Be quiet, you stuffy, pompous old bird! How dare you speak to me with such disrespect!' Mr Witty's smooth, plump cheeks were flushed with anger. 'You will apologise to me immediately!'

'Apologise? I don't think so, and we can all call each other names, Mr Witty, too witty, dim witty!' Cranlow hooted in derision.

Amidst the commotion, no-one noticed the figure who had entered the room and was regarding them with dismay, before making his presence known. Cranlow and the wizard continued to hurl insults at each other until a sound, like autumn leaves rustling in the wind, began to form into words.

'Enough! Cease this sniping at once!'

The words swished and swirled around the room, becoming louder and clearer, echoing backwards and forwards, filling every space and corner.

'Silence!'

As the sound of that final command slowly faded away, the figure emerged into the lamplight. They gasped in amazement as the Master of the Hall, the oldest and wisest of the wizards and one whom they knew to be immensely powerful, stood before them.

The Master surveyed the scene around him and blinked once in the direction of the remaining troublesome spells, causing them to hiss and splutter as they fizzled out, before turning his attention to a repentant young wizard, a disconcerted owl, the two trembling mice, and Wisp.

'This will not do.'

His voice, though deep and low, carried within it a hint of the sounds they had just heard.

'You, Cranlow, can be far too high and mighty for your own good, whilst you, Mr Witty, are at times careless and slapdash.'

He stared at each of them in turn as they hung their heads in shame. He seemed to tower over them, his cloak slowly changing colour from black to the deepest purple. His hair was as white as snow, as was the beard, which almost reached to his waist. Golden light edged his form as Wisp peeped up at him.

'And so it begins.' There was sadness in his voice. 'Come.'

He turned and swept out of the room. They followed, keeping close behind him, wondering what was going to happen next.

It was dark as they entered the chambers of the Master. He tapped the wall with his staff. Light instantly filled the room. He stood in front of them, his right hand slowly stroking his beard, before beckoning to Wisp.

'Come, youngster. Let me look at you. You must be the smallest of your kind I've ever seen, but you must grow quickly. You have such an important task ahead of you.'

'Pleathe, thir. What ith thith tathk you thpeak of?'

'Well may you ask, Wisp. Where to begin I wonder? Trouble has come to us. The wards are weakening, and the dark faerie are becoming strong again, threatening the balance of our worlds.'

'I met a fairy once,' said Robbit. 'Very pretty little creature she was too.'

'You were lucky then,' said the Master. 'You must take great care whenever you meet any kind of fairy, but these are not the same as the one you met. Oh no. These are from a very ancient tribe, malicious and dangerous, always seeking to do harm. It is these that we must deal with, and it will be a very difficult task indeed. Come. Let me show you.'

THE WATERS OF TRUTH

They followed the Master for what seemed like hours as he led them through winding passages, dark tunnels, and up and down countless flights of cold, stone steps until, at last, they stood in front of two massive panelled doors. The rough walls around them were covered in grime, yet the doors gleamed as if newly polished and oiled. On each panel a symbol was carved. A drum, a mirror, a raven, an owl, a flute, and a dragon.

'These doors were crafted from ancient oak trees many thousands of years ago. Every symbol holds a message which must be learned, but not now. First, we must ask permission to enter.' The Master rapped twice on the doors with his staff. 'The unworthy cannot enter here,' he said as he tapped each door again.

'Look. They're beginning to open,' said Wisp, moving forward.

'Wait,' said the Master. 'They must be fully open before we can enter or we may become trapped. There are rules here, which must be obeyed.'

As the doors slowly opened, they could see into a vast chamber. Mist rising up from the ground gradually disappeared as soft, yellow light illuminated a huge, underground cavern. The Master motioned them to follow as he made his way to its centre.

'This is the Place of Knowing,' he said in a hushed voice. 'You must see what it is that we have to deal with even though it will fill you with fear.'

They could hear the splash of water.

'This is what we seek.'

The Master led them towards a waterfall, which cascaded away into a seemingly bottomless chasm. As he approached, it moved sideways, revealing a smaller chamber beyond, in the middle of which stood a massive, stone bowl. The stone sparkled and glistened as if coated in ice. Steps led up to a platform from which they could look down into the cloudy water within it.

'Now we shall see. No one must speak. Not a sound, no matter what. Is that quite clear?'

He waited while they nodded their assent.

'These are the Waters of Truth,' he said sternly. 'Let's see what they have to tell us.'

He leaned over and touched the water with his staff. A faint glimmer of light briefly welled up from its depths as the surface began to clear. Creatures of nightmare moved through the water. Some resembled ugly, misshapen human forms. As they watched, the images became more distinct, revealing even worse horrors. The figures seemed to be dancing around something in their centre. Blood dripped from knives as they stabbed at it and from their hateful, sneering mouths. Slowly the object in the centre was revealed to them. It was a beautiful little girl.

The mice could not believe their eyes. They knew who she was. Pest could bear it no longer.

'No!' he cried out in dismay. 'Oh no!'

The Master quickly tried to end the awful sight, but not before one of the worst of them looked straight at Wisp, who, try as he might, could not look away. The tiny dragon sighed, as if all the breath were being drawn from his body, and collapsed onto the ground. The Master's staff flared with a fierce white light as he lifted the little dragon into his arms.

'We must leave here immediately, or we will lose him. They have their mark on him and will take him as he dreams. We must remove it, or he will be theirs for sure.'

They ran back towards the doors, stumbling in terror as the light faded behind them.

'Hurry!' shouted the Master. 'Before the doors bar our way!'

Fear and despair spurred them on. The Master stood between the doors, halting their closing just long enough for the last of them to squeeze through. As the doors shut behind them, they stood, panting and shaking, unable to move.

'There's not enough time,' said Robbit, looking at the limp figure of Wisp in the Master's arms. 'We'll never make it.'

'The House will take us. It has its own strange powers and can move both itself and us when needed. Come House, my chambers please,' he called, and after a momentary darkness, they found themselves back in the Master's rooms.

The wizard placed the unconscious little dragon into a golden cage.

'There now,' he said. 'That will hold them off for a while at least. They cannot touch the purity of gold. Besides, the cage holds a warding spell which will also help to keep them away.'

'What can we do now?' asked Mr Witty, sounding completely helpless.

'We need to find that cat,' replied the Master. 'He's very good at hiding when he's most needed. Go and get him House. Even he can't hide away from you.'

'Why him?' asked Pest. 'What can he do?'

'Well,' said the Master. 'There's more to him than what you see. He's a creature of magic, an elemental, a spirit of nature and a guardian. I know that's somewhat hard to believe, but he has chosen to serve our cause, so we must be very thankful as we certainly need his help.'

The House found Thomas admiring himself in front of a large oval mirror.

Not bad, he thought as he strutted backwards and forwards in front of it. *Not bad at all.*

He turned sideways to get a better look at himself.

'Nice shiny coat,' he purred. 'Not a hair out of place. Looking good.'

As he moved closer to the mirror to inspect his whiskers, two large eyes and a mouth appeared.

'Hey! What's going on? That's not me!'

'No, it isn't, is it?' said the mouth.

'Well, that's a relief. I knew I was better-looking than that.'

'Such vanity,' said the mouth. 'Anyway, playtime's over. You're wanted.'

'Wanted? Tell them I'm busy. Who wants me anyway?'

'The Master and none of your tricks this time. Hang on to your hat, cat, you're about to fly.'

'I haven't got a hat.'

'Well, hang on to your whiskers then. Hang on tight.'

And with that, the House flew Thomas at lightning speed towards the Master, knowing that if given half a chance, the cat would change into his elemental form, and then it really would be impossible to track him down.

FIGHTING FOR WISP

'Ah. So you've finally decided to grace us with your presence.'

Thomas skidded across the floor, bumped into a chair and narrowly missed colliding with the leg of a table before coming to a stop at the Master's feet.

'This House is trying to kill me. How I've escaped serious injury to my person I shall never know.'

'That,' said the Master, 'is quite a mystery to each and every one of us. However, you are here now and all in one piece, so let's get on, shall we?'

Thomas spotted Wisp lying inside the golden cage.

'What's that pesky little worm doing in there?'

'That pesky little worm, as you call him, is in serious danger. He's been marked by one of the Vakralla and we need your help to save him.'

'Oh. Well, isn't that just great? That's all we need. What was he doing to attract their attention anyway? Finally made himself invisible to all of us and appeared to them instead?'

'No! It wasn't like that, you nasty old cat!' shouted Pest. 'And if you don't stop all your talking, our poor little friend could die!'

Thomas glared at the mouse.

'Well. Aren't we brave today? As if we didn't have enough problems without having to listen to your squeaky comments as well.'

It was Cranlow's turn to speak. The owl had been remarkably quiet up to now.

23

'I think that what has happened should be a dire warning to us all and instead of arguing, we should call a truce and try to be civil to each other.'

'Well done, Cranlow,' said the Master. 'I couldn't have said it better. Now, let us begin, while there is still time.'

'Excuse me, Mr Owl, sir,' said Robbit. 'Please, may I ask you something?'

'You may,' hooted Cranlow, still sounding very haughty.

'Would we really have given you indigestion if you'd eaten us?'

The Master looked at Cranlow and tutted loudly as he said.

'You're going to come crashing down to earth with such a wallop one of these days. You may be thankful to eat bugs later, so be careful what you say from now on, *Mister* Owl.'

Cranlow muttered something that sounded like 'Oh. Ooh. Yes. Quite.' Hopped from one foot to the other then closed his great, hooded eyes.

'Well, I hate to butt in here, but something's happening to that there dragon.' Thomas pointed to the cage.

Wisp was glowing with a soft, creamy light. His body had changed from grey to the colour of the whitest pearl.

'It has begun,' said the Master. 'But he is strong for one so small. See how he fights them. Thomas, it is time for you to do your part. You must become the true elemental being that you are and enter into the spirit of our small friend. There you must help him in the battle for his life. Mr Witty, we must summon the four elements of which we are all a part; earth, air, water, and fire. Cranlow, you will preside over the air, and you two mice will stand near the place of the earth. You must stand your ground. Do not enter the circle. Your only protection is to remain outside.'

As the wizard began to chant, the room became darker and colder. Strange sounds could be heard coming from the circle of magic he had created. The sounds became louder. They could hear screaming and shouting, the din of fighting and the clash of swords. Thunder rolled, and lightning flashed all around them. Suddenly, the figure of a woman materialised in front of the Master. She was tall, her long, straight hair as dark as the wings of a bat. She moved towards him, glaring at him through eyes filled with cruelty and spite. He pointed his staff towards her, and it blazed with the same intense, white light as at the Waters of Truth.

'Begone!' he cried. 'Return to the realm to which you are bound!'

The woman sneered at him.

'Fool of a wizard. Do you really think you can hold us? We are Vakralla. Soon nothing will stop us. Then we will come for you. I give you the wyrm. Have him for now. It will make no difference. We will bind him to us when we regain our rightful place in this world.'

The Master struck the ground with his staff. All the colours of the rainbow swirled around him as he moved towards the woman, who retreated from him, shielding her eyes from the brightness.

'Go, foul creature of darkness! Go! Back to the abyss where you belong!'

She stopped and hissed into the face of the wizard. Blood dripped from her mouth and sizzled as it splashed onto the hem of his gown. He struck her with his staff. She screamed as the illusion of beauty shattered and she stood before them in the frightful shape of her true identity, before disappearing as suddenly as she had come.

'They,' said the voice of the cat, 'really are one nasty lot.'

'Thomas?' called Robbit. 'Where is he? I can't see him anywhere.'

'Here,' said Thomas. 'Or I could be over there. In fact, I could be just anywhere.'

'Don't worry about him,' said Cranlow. 'Thinks he's clever, but I know where he is. Sixth sense, you know.'

'What about Wisp?' asked Pest. 'Is he all right now?'

And as he heard the friendly voice, the little dragon cried out, 'Hallo. Hallo. What am I doing in here? Help, pleathe, thomeone.'

The Master lifted Wisp out of the golden cage. 'Well done, little one. You've beaten them this time.'

'Don't forget me. I've been in there too.'

Thomas appeared in front of them. His usually silky, black coat was in total disarray. There were bald patches on his back, and across his left shoulder an even larger patch where his fur had turned silver.

'Never again,' he grumbled as he left them. 'Don't ever expect me to do that again. Just look at this coat. My appearance is ruined. It's going to take me forever to sort this out. Oh dear. Oh goodness me. This is just too much!'

'Let's hope he's a long way off when he discovers the white bit,' said Robbit. 'That will really give him something to moan about.'

Wisp was looking very confused as the Master explained what had happened.

'What you saw in the pool was an image of what could happen if the faerie ever came back into this world. You were very lucky, Wisp. They are an unthinkable threat. Even though they appear to be beautiful, they are vampires thirsty for blood. Now you have been touched by one of them, you will be known by them all. However, your own magic will help you to know if they are near, and until you are bigger and stronger, you must be very careful indeed.'

'But I saw the little girl,' said Pest. 'They were hurting her.'

'No,' said the Master. 'But the danger is real. We must—and will—make sure that they never get their detestable hands on her.'

'She is the child from the house on the edge of the woods,' said Cranlow. 'I've seen her playing in the garden.'

'Why do they want her?' asked Wisp.

'Well,' began the Master. 'Ever since the Vakralla, amongst others of their kind, were banished from this world long, long ago, the ancient wisdom of our ancestors has been hidden. The only way to keep it safe was to bury it deep within the memories of a chosen family.

'None knew the secret they possessed. And so the magic of that wisdom was forgotten, only to be reawakened in the most dire of circumstances. It is that which is upon us now. The brother of this little girl is such a one. Within his memory, buried deep, lies the most powerful magic of all. These evil faerie wish to capture her and once ensnared, use her to lure James into their clutches. They will stop at nothing to possess the secret that he holds. But believe me, those are not the worst of them. They do the bidding of the darkest power the earth has ever known. Something has happened, and we must find out what it is without delay because if they ever become powerful again, it could mean the end of us all.'

DANGEROUS SECRETS

Daisy waved to James as he approached the cottage. The woman bent down and patted the cat on its head.

'Well done, Thomas. More good deeds like this will help you to get your coat back into shape, but it'll take quite a while, I think.'

She turned to James.

'Don't worry my dear. Daisy's fine and ready for bed—aren't you, child?'

Daisy nodded and ran to James who picked her up, relief flooding through him.

'Who are you?' he asked. 'Where are we? How will our parents know how to find us?'

'No need to worry about your parents,' said the woman. 'You just leave them to me. My name is Mrs Fellows, and as to who I am, let's just say I was a friend of your grandmother. Isn't that right, Tom?'

'You could say that, I suppose,' said the cat.

James stared at it in amazement. 'Cats don't talk. Cats can't talk.'

'Who said cats don't talk? I'm not just your average old cat, you know. I, am something completely different.'

'You can say that again,' said the woman. 'There is most certainly not another one like you, Thomas.'

'Will someone please tell me what's going on?' James pleaded as she encouraged him inside.

'Come and eat, James. You must be very hungry after your ordeal. Then you must rest and sleep. It's too late now. We'll talk about it all in the morning.'

The strangeness of the situation had dampened James's appetite, but he did his best with the food Mrs Fellows provided before being shown to his room. He woke late the next morning and jumped out of bed, confused and concerned, before rushing into the kitchen to find breakfast laid out and Daisy sitting in the armchair next to the fire, hugging the cat.

'I like it here,' she said. 'And Mrs Fellows is a very nice lady.'

'That's all very well,' replied James. 'But Mum and Dad must be out of their minds with worry by now. They've probably got the police out looking for us.'

'Naw,' said the cat. 'Won't have even noticed you're gone.'

'How can you say that?' asked James, wondering why he was having a conversation with a cat.

'Because of time,' said Thomas, who had shaken himself free from Daisy's cuddles and was about to leave the room.

'Don't you go walking off,' said James in alarm. 'What's this about time?'

Thomas jumped up onto the chair next to James. 'Well. Let me see. In some places like your world, time passes real fast, and if I were there, I could end up getting old. My sleek, black coat could start to fall out and turn white all over. Spoil my looks real bad.' Thomas stared at James. 'You still don't get it, do you? I thought you were supposed to be bright. The fact is, you're not in your world now. You're in mine. Time's different here. That's why, when you get back home, no-one will have missed you. Worked it out yet?'

'You're telling me that time stands still here?' asked James. 'Well, that just can't happen except in fairy stories, so what are you trying to say?'

'I give up,' said the cat. 'Ask her.' He turned towards Mrs Fellows, who was listening from the doorway. 'Mrs Fellows is a witch, and if she can't convince you, no-one can.'

'Wise woman, Tom. Not so much of the witch.'

James was beginning to think he was going mad.

'So, if what you're saying is true and you don't grow old, why have you got that big patch of white fur on your shoulder? What's that all about?'

'That,' said Thomas, 'has got nothing to do with it.'

'That's it,' said James, standing up and holding out his hand to his sister. 'Come on, Daisy. We're going home. Right now!'

Mrs Fellows looked at them both. Her face was sad.

'I'm so sorry, James, but it's not that simple. You and I need to talk, and Tom can take Daisy for a nice walk in the garden, can't you, Tom?'

'Why do you keep calling me Tom? You know that's not my name.'

'Because I like it, and because you keep calling me *witch*.'

The cat spluttered and rolled his eyes to the ceiling before leading Daisy out.

'Well,' Mrs Fellows began, 'when I said I was a friend of your grandmother James, what I really meant was your great-grandmother. I am her second cousin. So we are family. And as such, we have an inherited knowledge. The powers we possess are handed down through each generation of the family. We are the guardians, the trusted caretakers, of a great secret, but only one person holds the key to unlocking that secret. And that person James, is you. You, are the Keeper.'

James was beginning to feel sick. This woman didn't look any older than his mother. His voice was small and weak as he asked, 'Keeper? I don't understand.'

'Whatever happens in this world affects your world too. If bad things happen here, they sort of leak through, upsetting the balance of everything, causing disorder and chaos. It has happened before, in a time almost lost to our memory. Then, formidable, ancient knowledge was used to stop the deadly fiends, but they are breaking through the magic that binds them. They are determined to possess the key to their freedom. The key, which you hold, James, can either give them back that freedom or lock them away forever.'

James sat with his head in his hands, trying not to burst into tears. *This isn't happening*, he thought.

'I'm afraid it is, James,' said Mrs Fellows, reading his thoughts rather alarmingly. 'Try not to be afraid. There are many here who will help you, but first we have to make sure that Daisy is safe. They have already sent one of their watchers to draw her to them. They will do everything in their power to get to you. The noise you thought you heard in her bedroom was one of their Vraga. A bloodthirsty monster, as they are. He's the fairy man she thinks is her friend.'

James shuddered. Something told him this was no joke. Yet surely there was no way it could be true, and he didn't want anything to do with it.

'No!' he cried. 'I just want to go home. This is all a whole load of nonsense and I don't believe any of it!' His fear was making him angry.

'I'm so sorry, James, but you really have no other options. You've got to take this seriously. Both you and your sister are in terrible danger. If this dark power rises again, it will destroy us all.'

'Why me? What do you expect me to do?' He was shouting, and his whole body was starting to shake. 'I can't do anything, can I?'

'Yes, James, you can, and we will help you. You must talk to the Master, along with others who will assist you, especially the one they call Wisp.'

'So where is this Master and the rest of them then?'

'They are almost here,' she said mysteriously. 'The House of Wizards is bringing them to us. Don't look so puzzled—you've always known of its existence. It's the house you and your friends were always looking for but could never find.'

As she spoke, the room seemed to tilt. James felt a shudder run through the floor and hung on to the table for support. He felt as if he was turning and spinning, a bit like being on the waltzers at the fair. The movement stopped as suddenly as it had started. James was so giddy he almost fell over.

'Oops. Sorry about that. Have to make a few adjustments for next time.'

The voice filled the room, coming from no-where in particular but filling everywhere with sound.

'Don't even bother,' said Thomas. 'Just admit you've lost the plot. It's a miracle we all arrive in one piece as it is.'

'I don't do miracles,' said the voice. 'Miracles are not part of my job description.'

Thomas shook his head as he turned to James. 'Let me introduce you to the House. It's a bit of a moaner, but it's not a bad traveller. It hasn't actually lost us yet, even though its landings aren't up to much.'

'Did I hear a compliment there? Did you actually say something nice about me? Well, I am amazed. I could even pretend that you're good-looking. Well, perhaps not. Now that really would take a miracle.'

As the voice slowly faded away, a tall figure approached from out of the shadows.

'It's the Master,' whispered Thomas.

The imposing presence seemed to float across the floor. Glittering spangles trimmed the hem of his long, crimson robe. As James waited in trepidation, a name formed in his mind: Kallen Lupus.

'Ah. I see you have remembered my name. Very good. Your memories will reveal themselves when the time is right. Don't be afraid, James. You have nothing to fear from us. We are all quite harmless, aren't we?'

Robbit and Pest squeaked their hellos, followed by Mr Witty, who was now wearing an orange feather in the band of his hat.

Cranlow hovered at eye level in front of James as he hooted, 'Good afternoon, dear boy. So nice to have you with us, I'm sure.'

James was speechless in his amazement.

'Don't forget me. Pleathe let me thay hello too.'

'This,' said Thomas, 'is Wisp. A dragon. Well, that's what he tells us he is. If you believe that, you'll believe anything. Wisp? A wisp of what? Smoke, perhaps? Can't even do that, can you?'

'Be careful,' said the Master. 'You won't think it so funny when he can.'

They turned at the sound of Daisy's voice as Mrs Fellows led her into the room.

'Will you play with me?' she asked Wisp, as she sat on the floor in front of him. They all laughed. The Master beckoned to the cat.

'Much to do I think Thomas. But for now, we will leave them to enjoy each other's company, before their ordeal must begin.'

EMMA NO MATES

James needed to talk to his dad. Something had happened, but he couldn't think what it was. His head ached and he had slept badly. He hesitated before knocking on the door of his father's study. As usual, there was no reply, so he decided to go in anyway. His father was sitting at his desk, staring out into the garden. James could make out from his expression that he wasn't actually seeing anything. He stood in front of him, unsure of what to say. All he wanted was some comfort, a smile, a hug, a word to make him feel that everything was going to be OK.

'Dad?' he ventured.

Yet his father hadn't moved. His expression was blank. James tried again. He didn't know whether to shout or cry. He put his hand on his father's arm and stared directly into his face. His father didn't seem to know he was there. James shook him, overcome by his growing anger and frustration.

'Please, Dad. It's me. Jamie. Speak to me! Please, Dad.'

There was no response. James sat and stared at his father, desperate for a sign of acknowledgement, but there was no change, so he left, slamming the door behind him.

Getting to school had been a blur, and he'd taken his chance to escape just after assembly, making his way to the seafront. Not knowing what else to do, he wandered aimlessly along the pier. He was sad, confused, deeply hurt, and feeling very helpless and alone.

'Day off from school then?'

This girl was following him. He was sure of it. He saw her nearly everywhere he went, lurking about in the background. She was standing next to the ice cream van, hands pushed deep into the pockets of her scruffy jeans. Emma Jenkins. Emma 'No Mates' Jenkins. He shook his head and glared at her. She pretended to be interested in something on the ground in front of her as he made a point of ignoring her, hoping she'd take the hint and go away. But she was having none of it.

'Well?' she asked.

'No! What's it to you anyway?'

'Nothin'.'

'So why ask then? And you can talk. You're no goody-goody, are you? Go on! Get lost!' James felt anger boiling up inside him. He knew it wasn't her fault, but he felt helpless and out of control.

'Why should I? Don't you tell me what to do, Jamie Cadwallader! Not so clever now, are you!'

'Go away!' he shouted, pushing her. 'Get away from me!'

She fell against the iron railings which edged the sea wall. There were tears in her eyes as she picked herself up.

'I'll get you for this!'

Her face was flushed with temper, and she was shouting.

'It's not my fault! It's not my fault your dad's gone batty!'

She ran down the steps and onto the beach stopping just below him, kicking at the sand. A mass of unkempt, curly, chestnut coloured hair hung down over her tear-streaked face. She pushed it back and held it on the top of her head as she squinted up at him.

'Mm. Well. I didn't really mean that. You know, about your dad. I just got a bit cross. Sorry. I only wanted to talk to you. If you're not going in to school, you'd better go where no-one will see you. Yeah?'

He nodded, trying not to feel the pain welling up inside him, making his chest hurt and his throat tight. His head felt as if it were going to explode. Tears choked him as he jumped down onto the sand and ran, tripping and stumbling across the beach towards the sea.

The tide was going out. Waves frothed and bubbled over the warm sand, leaving a trail of bright-green seaweed and broken shells. Emma was sitting on a rock at the water's edge. She'd followed him.

'You OK?'

He shrugged, as a wave splashed over his feet.

'Your shoes are getting wet.'

'So what.' He walked further into the water.

'Is your dad really ill then?'

'Dunno.'

The water was cold. The rocks were warm and dry.

He sat down next to her and said, 'You don't like school, do you?'

She half turned away from him. 'Nope.'

'You must like aggro then.'

'Oh yeah.'

Her voice was very subdued. He didn't know what to say.

'They can't make me go. Anyway, I'll just run away. Done it before. They don't care.'

She stood up and stretched before finding some money in her pocket.

'You wanna lemonade or something?'

'Stress,' he said, forcing the words out. 'My dad. Something like that, I think. I'm not really sure.'

She waited for him as he followed her up the beach towards the nearby cafe'.

'Hey look!' she called out, pointing. 'There's your cat. I like cats, 'specially black ones. Come on, puss. Puss. Puss!'

'It's not mine.' The cat was staring at him. It had a patch of white fur on its left shoulder.

'Well it must like you, Jamie. It follows you everywhere.'

'Just like you then, and don't call me Jamie.'

Emma grinned.

REMEMBERING NONSENSE

'Look at me, James. I'm speaking to you!' His mother was very angry. 'Why weren't you at school today? Don't you think we've got enough problems at the moment? Why are you behaving like this?'

James looked at the ceiling.

'Don't do that! You weren't brought up to be rude, were you?'

He shook his head.

'Right! Well, this has got to stop. You are distressing your father. He's becoming very worried about you and so am I.

'So why doesn't he ever speak to me then? He never does anything any more. Just shuts himself up in his study.'

'He's not well, James.' There was a catch in her voice. 'You know he's not himself. We're all trying to make the best of what's happened. Can't you at least try to understand?'

'Understand what? How can I understand when nobody tells me anything? All I ever hear is "Not now James." "Turn the music down, James." "Be quiet, James." I can't even have my friends round now either.'

'Yes. Well, this isn't all about you. It's about time you realised that and tried not to be so selfish.'

'I'm not selfish!'

His mother's face was a blur as the tears stung his eyes. He lurched out of the kitchen, kicking the door open. He felt like punching something. What was it Emma had said? 'I'll just run away. Then they'll be sorry.' Selfish? How could she say that? He looked back at the house and saw the cat sitting on the kitchen windowsill. His mother hadn't noticed it. The cat yawned and stretched as it watched him. He leaned on the garden wall and stared back at it. The cat's unblinking gaze was beginning to make him feel uncomfortable. A strange sense of dread made him shiver, and somewhere, in the back of his mind, a vague memory stirred. Something to do with a cat that could talk? *Rubbish*, he thought. *Cats don't talk. And all that stuff about magic and wizards? It's just absolutely ridiculous.* Daisy was full of it, of course. The dragon story was her favourite. He sighed. Poor Daisy. She was upset too, especially now that Mum couldn't spend so much time with her. She'd been telling everyone about a funny little man with orange hair and a red hat. At first she'd said she liked him, but now she said he was horrid. Mum said it was Daisy's way of getting attention.

It was about three weeks since his father had been brought home from the office. He hadn't been to work or anywhere else since. Auntie Caroline, his dad's sister, had mentioned something about a breakdown and that he could be like it for ages. They all stopped talking if they thought his dad could hear them. No one talked to James either. Not properly. What even was a 'breakdown'?

The cat jumped down from the windowsill and sat in front of him. 'A *talking* cat?' The thought made him smile. '*Hilarious*' He started to walk back towards the house.

'See ya.'

He stopped. There was no way he was going to turn around. The hairs on the back of his neck were tingling with goosebumps. He frowned. Better say sorry to Mum.

Daisy was standing in her bedroom doorway, watching her mother spraying air freshener under the bed and behind the cupboards.

'There, that should do it. No more nasty smells in here.' She looked at Daisy and smiled.

'What's up?' James screwed up his face. 'Ugh! That smells awful. Was it you, Dais?'

His mother laughed.

'I think there must be something wrong with the drains. Do me a favour, James. Take your sister out for a bit, will you? Give me a chance to do some jobs.'

'Well. OK,' he said reluctantly, knowing he couldn't get out of it. 'Come on then, Dais. Get you out in the fresh air. Blow the pong away.'

His mother looked back at them on her way down the stairs, noticing the expression on Daisy's face.

'Oh dear. You've done it now, James. Better go quick. *We* are not amused.'

Daisy peered up at James, her face wearing her most serious 'I don't think you're funny' look.

'Oh, come on, Dais. I'm not laughing. Honest. See?' He knelt down in front of her.

'Yes, you are. You are. Your face thinks it's funny.'

'Well, all right. Sorry. I know it wasn't really you.'

She pulled his head closer to her and whispered in his ear, 'But I know who did it.'

'You do? Who was it then?' he asked, trying not to giggle.

'It's that man. You know. The one with the red hat and the horrid hair. He smells.' She held her nose. 'Yuck!'

Her breath tickled his ear. He felt uneasy. It was there again, that feeling, the feeling that something weird was happening. Of something prowling in the shadows. Something waiting, hungry and impatient. Daisy was shaking him.

'Look, James. Look. The cat has come to see us.'

She put her arms around its neck and hugged it tight.

'This child is trying to strangle me!'

The cat *was* talking.

'Well, don't just stand there. Get her off.'

As James freed the cat, Daisy stamped her foot at him.

'He's not yours. I want him!'

'He's not yours either, Daisy. Why don't you ask him if he's got a name?'

'You may know me as Thomas. That will do for now.'

Daisy put her arms around the cat again.

'You can come with us, can't he, James? And we can get ice cream and go to the swings?'

James groaned. He had to say yes. It wasn't her fault everything was going wrong; anyway, she made him laugh, and he wanted to get out of the house.

'Oh, come on then,' he replied. 'But only if you stop choking that cat.'

Emma found them at the swings.

'Doing your good deed for the day then?'

She sat on the swing next to Daisy.

'Give us a push, Jamie. Your cat's here again, I see.'

'It's not mine, and I wish it would go back where it came from.'

'What? And miss out on my brilliant company?'

'Who said that?' Emma looked around her and then at James.

'I know who it was.' Daisy was leaning back in her swing, a big blob of ice cream on her nose and a knowing look on her face. 'It's Thomas.'

'Thomas? Who's Thomas? We're the only ones here.' Emma stared at Daisy, who was pointing at the cat.

'It's him. It is. He can talk.' She was nodding her head. 'Tell her, James. Tell her.'

'Yes James. Why don't you? I'll just introduce myself, seeing as you've lost the plot. Hi. I'm Thomas. Better close your mouth before a big, fat, old fly comes buzzing in. You'll just love getting to know me. Won't she, James?'

'If you say so, and if she can put up with your boasting. Still over the top, I see.'

What am I saying?' James thought. *How could this be happening? I've got to be dreaming.*

'Over the top! Me! Never! And no, James, you aren't dreaming. This is real. I'm going to talk to Emma while you take Daisy home. And please be quick about it. We haven't got much time. Make sure you're back here by six o'clock. You've got a very important appointment with the Seer. Make no mistake, James, you're going to need all the help you can get.'

James didn't want to move. He looked at Emma, who was speechless.

'The dreams are real, James. The fear you feel is a warning of the danger to come. But don't forget, you've got me here to help you. This just has to be your lucky day.' For all his joking, the cat sounded deadly serious.

James sighed in disbelief.

'All right! But how am I supposed to know anything when I can't remember what I'm supposed to be dreaming?'

'Not remember?'

The cat strutted up and down in front of them, bristling with irritation.

'Of course you can. Do try and concentrate, James. I don't like having to repeat myself. There's no way you could have forgotten me. And what about that other useless lot? They're all here now too. Those two scatterbrained mice are in your house. Remember them? No? Can't say I blame you. They're calling themselves spies. Supposed to be keeping an eye on things and reporting back. That snooty owl Cranlow's been hooting about in the woods. He's even more full of himself now than ever. Lost his specs the other day and ended up flapping about in the church. Thought it was a barn. Nearly gave the vicar a heart attack.'

The cat was really enjoying this.

'What a dunderhead. Speaking of which, Mr Witty, that twit of a wizard, is blundering about somewhere. I did my best to get rid of him, but the Master wouldn't listen. Oh, yes. I nearly forgot. How could I? The so-called dragon. Every time he speaks, he sets fire to something. No control. And here I am, trying to keep my cool, and I'm sent off to fight the most dangerous battle ever with a gang of good-for-nothing nit wits. Except you, James . . . and myself of course.'

As he listened, James tried to dig deeper into his memory, but everything was hazy and unclear. Somehow he knew that what lay hidden there was not his to control. Daisy was stroking the cat as she asked. 'Can we give Thomas some nice milk when we get home?'

He nodded, taking hold of his sister's hand as he said.

'Nice milk for the pussycat?'

Thomas turned his back on him.

'If you're going to be hanging around the house, you'd better not let our mum catch you. She can't stand cats.'

Daisy nodded. 'She said they was 'sgusting 'cause they ate all the little birds.'

Thomas was inspecting his claws.

'Rubbish,' he said. 'That's completely absurd. Your mother will just love me. You wait and see. Everybody loves me. How could they not? There'd have to be something wrong with them.'

'You coming then?'

'No,' Thomas replied without looking at James. 'Not just now. See you later, and make sure you're not late.'

MEETING MR FAIRWEATHER

Some girls were hanging about near the swings, but there was no sign of Emma, or the cat. James checked his watch. It was nearly six o'clock. He caught a fleeting movement amongst the bushes at the edge of the lake and turned quickly. There was no one there. They had let him down.

What am I supposed to do now? he thought.

'Jamie!' Emma was running towards him, her arms waving.

'Where were you? I was just going.'

She was out of breath. 'Sorry. Some woman from social services wanted to see me. Couldn't get away. Anyway, I'm here now, so what's going on?'

'Don't ask me. I haven't got a clue. It's that blinking cat. He's so full of it and then can't be bothered to turn up.'

'So it's true then, all that weird stuff. I still can't believe it.'

'I wish I didn't. I'm trying not to. Hang on. What's that noise? Can you hear bells?'

She nodded.

'It's the local Morris dancers. They come here to practise. Haven't you seen them before? They're all a bit eccentric, I think. Well, they'd have to be, wouldn't they, to carry on like that? Fancy a good laugh?'

The dancers were just about to start. Surreal designs in black and white paint covered their faces. It looked as if they were wearing masks. On their heads they wore an assortment of hats and feathers some of which had tails of shiny tinsel or gaudy, patterned scarves and ribbons which hung down their backs. Their rag coats were made up of tatters of brightly coloured strips of cloth and were more like cloaks than coats. On each leg, just below the knee, they wore the bells James had heard. In front of them stood a tall man who was about to play an accordion. Next to him sat a small, bearded man whose clothes, face and tall, top hat, were all so black, he looked like an imp. On his lap he held a drum. A fiddle player was tuning up next to him.

'Are we ready?' The tall man signalled them to start.

Emma nudged James. 'Wait for it. They'll start beating themselves up with sticks in a minute.'

With a look of glee her face, she started to mimic them, slowly at first then faster as she copied their movements.

'Come on, James.'

The music seemed louder.

'Come on.' She pulled him towards them.

All James could hear were the bells, the sharp clack of the striking sticks, and the throb of the drum keeping time. The dancers surrounded him, drawing him in, their feet beating out the rhythm of the earth as they traced the time-worn steps of the dance. The power of the drum increased, quivering through him. He began to feel dizzy as they carried him with them, their rag coats becoming a kaleidoscope of whirling colour and light. Faster and faster they turned, lifting him into the heart of the dance, lulling him, soothing him, as he felt himself falling into the light.

Emma was scared. James could tell by the way she was biting her lip and the fact that she couldn't keep still. She noticed him looking at her and tried to smile.

Where am I? What happened?'

'Ah. At last we have you.'

It was the accordion man. He had washed the paint off his face but still wore the comical hat and the rag coat.

'Who are you?' James asked. 'What's going on?'

Emma grabbed hold of James and pulled.

'Let's go! Now! I don't like it.'

She had dragged James to his feet.

'Come on, James. Run!'

'It's all right,' said the man. 'You've nothing to be afraid of from me.'

Emma was standing behind James.

'So why are we here then?'

He could feel her trembling as she tried to get him to move.

'Don't listen to him James. ' Now she was shouting. 'I know all about people like you! Just you let us out of here now!'

'You may come and go as you please. Truly, I wish you no harm, and I can help you if you'll let me. I was hoping to meet you both earlier.'

'Were you?' asked James. 'So who are you? I was supposed to meet someone in the park, but they didn't show up.' Emma was still tugging at his arm.

'Yes, I know. Unfortunately, things didn't quite go as planned. But never mind. You're here now. Let me introduce myself. Fairweather, Adrian Fairweather.'

He held out his hand in greeting. James hesitated before shaking it. 'Are you the Seer?' he asked.

'Seer? Well, that's what they call me, so I suppose I am. Sorry about the way you got here. Bit of a problem, you see. No alternative, I'm afraid.'

'What kind of a problem?' Emma was beginning to calm down.

Well, it really is a pity you didn't get here sooner, James. Would have given us a fighting chance, so to speak. I'm going on a bit, aren't I? Now where was I? Oh, yes. The fact is, you're being followed.'

James gave a sigh of relief.

'Yes, I know but it's not a problem. That cat's been following me around for ages. I just can't get rid of it.'

Mr Fairweather looked very sad.

'It's not him. I wish it were that simple. No. What follows you comes from beyond death itself. You and your sister are in the most awful peril. Its strength is growing fast, and soon it will be too late.' He looked at Emma. 'If you help James, you must understand that this is deadly serious. Anyone who stands against this could pay with their life.'

Emma's eyes were huge as the blood drained from her face.

'That cat said that something really bad was going to happen.'

She looked at James for reassurance. He made a wry face and shook his head.

Mr Fairweather sighed.

'Well, my dear. How can I tell you? James is the key to all this. He holds a very important secret.' He turned to James, 'And you have no idea what I'm talking about, do you?'

James didn't bother to reply. Mr Fairweather gave him a long, questioning look.

'Just as I thought. Now then, where was I? Ah yes. What if I told you that once, a very long time ago, fairies and humans all lived together? You'd find that hard to imagine, wouldn't you? Anyway, all was well until trouble started in the realm of a certain fairy tribe. Fighting broke out amongst them, and the evil that was driving them began to spread. It killed anyone who stood in its path. Darkness followed it, like a foul, black plague, devouring everything as it swept across the land.'

He paused and took a deep breath. His face was troubled.

'So what's this got to do with James?'

'Be patient, child. There is still more to tell. Every day, the evil power increased. Great cities were destroyed. No life survived. The monstrous demon feasted on fear and pain. It drank the blood of all those slain and left their bones to rot upon the ground. All the remaining power of the fairy realms and the human world was used up in one last desperate attempt to stop it. Finally, it was defeated, together with its vile followers, to be bound forever behind the furthermost gate of the realm of Nowhere.'

James had a sinking feeling in the pit of his stomach.

'Are they still there?'

Mr Fairweather shook his head.

'That, my dear James, is the problem. The magic that binds them is weakening. They are beginning to break free. A human family were entrusted with the knowledge that could stop them. You, James, are a direct descendant of that family. You are the Keeper. You hold the key to their destruction, the secret that has been passed down through the generations.'

Emma couldn't keep quiet any longer.

'So what is it, James? What's this secret? Let's hear it then'

'He doesn't know. It's hidden deep in his mind. He can only find it with the help of a certain dragon and then only when the time is right. Don't look so sad, James. All is far from lost. We still have some tricks up our sleeve. While we can still breathe, we can fight! Eh?' Mr Fairweather was trying to sound convincing.

'Yes, but how? What are we going to do? Weren't you supposed to tell me something important?'

'Me? Important? Hm. What was it now? Ah. I've got it.'

He drew a small, black velvet bag from his pocket.

'These things can change by the minute, you know.'

He shook the bag three times before handing it to James.

'Your turn. Three shakes, then give it back to me.'

The bag felt much heavier than it looked. Mr Fairweather opened it.

'Put your hand in and take out the one that comes to you.'

'How will I know that?'

The Seer smiled. 'You just will.'

James put his hand into the bag. Nothing happened. He closed his eyes and concentrated. Mr Fairweather laughed.

'You can't make it happen, James.'

Then something moved inside the bag. He tried to take his hand out, but it wouldn't budge. He felt a prickling sensation as his fingers closed over the object pushing into his palm. It was a highly polished stone, about the size of a large coat button with a strange mark etched into its surface. James handed it to the Seer.

'More,' said Mr. Fairweather. 'We need to look at them all.'

'Why can't we just tip them out all at once?'

'Because they need to sort of tune into you so we can get a proper reading. Lay them down in a circle and put the last one in the middle.'

'How many are there?' asked Emma.

'Twenty-five. Don't worry. It won't take long. Come along, James. Come along.'

Eventually, James laid out the last one and stepped back from the table. His hand was hurting. He rubbed it against his leg.

'What are they?' he asked as the Seer leaned over them.

'What? Oh, these. Sorry. They're runes. Have a good look at them. If you want to move them about or take some away, better do it now. No? Well then, let's see what we've got.'

He paced around them, humming and haaing, backwards and forwards, tutting and tchawing. He pursed his lips and sucked his teeth, scratched his head and tapped his feet. James heard Emma squeak. He turned to look at her and started to giggle. The sight of Mr Fairweather hopping and huffing around the table like an overstuffed pantomime turkey was just too much. Every few minutes, he stopped, poked his head forward, then held his hand up as if he were about to speak. Each time made them laugh even more. Emma was crying.

'Do something,' she said. 'I can't stand it.'

Suddenly, Mr Fairweather clapped his hands and stood absolutely still.

'What?'

James felt weak and was still giggling.

'Come here, my boy. What's the joke, by the way? I could do with a good laugh. Well, perhaps not. Let me tell you what the runes have to say. It's as we thought. Your enemies are gathering and coming ever closer. You are about to begin a very dangerous journey. You must rely on your friends and trust the one who calls himself Thomas. The Keeper of the Stones will start you on your way. And then there is the other problem. Look at the stone in the middle.'

James looked. The runic marking looked like the number 1. It meant nothing to him. He shook his head.

'It represents ice. It is the rune that speaks of problems and arguments. The loss of friends and trouble in the family. A deathly cold that will numb your body and freeze your mind.'

James was feeling uncomfortable. He turned to Emma, but she wouldn't look at him.

'Will my dad get better?'

Mr Fairweather sighed.

'I can't say, James. There is nothing here that says he won't. I think your father's problems have a lot to do with what's happening. Time will tell, my boy. Time will tell.'

'Why is this happening to me? Why can't things be like they were before? I don't want to be a part of all this.' James felt tired and weak.

'Hot chocolate. That'll do it.' Mr Fairweather beckoned to Emma. 'Come along, my dear, you can help. Sit down, James. We'll soon have you feeling better.'

Emma nodded. 'Have you got any biscuits or cake and stuff? I'm starving.'

The Seer had cinnamon cake, gooey caramel slices, and blueberry muffins washed down with more sweet, hot chocolate. James was stuffed. He pushed his plate away from him, shaking his head at the offer of more.

'Who is this Keeper of the Stones? How will we know where to find him?'

'You know him already. He's the man you see tidying up the beach and rearranging the stones along the sea wall.'

'You've got to be joking,' said Emma. 'It can't be him. He's really creepy.'

'Not everything is as it seems, my girl. I know him very well, and I certainly don't think he's creepy.' Mr Fairweather was smiling. 'A bit strange, maybe, but definitely not creepy. Anyhow, you must find out for yourselves. His name is Michael.'

James wasn't convinced.

'Is that it then? Isn't there anything else you need to tell us, like what's going to happen next?'

'No. Nothing I can think of at the moment. Would you like some more cake? No? Well, just take care on the way home. Oh. Yes. I'll find you when we need to speak again. Don't worry, James. I'm a bit like that cat—there's more to me than meets the eye, which reminds me. I must speak to him about the use of certain words. Dunderhead, indeed!'

A GIFT OF STONE

'I don't really want you going out again this afternoon, James.'

His mother had her back to him as she spoke. She was looking out of the window to where his father was leaning on the gate at the bottom of the garden.

'What's he doing out there? Why won't he talk to me?'

'He's ill James. I'm sure he doesn't mean it. He can't help the way he is at the moment, and you're not helping.'

'But he's just making it worse. He isn't even trying. It's as if he doesn't care any more.'

'He's going to see the doctor tomorrow. Perhaps that will help. I don't know why you have to be so difficult.' She folded her arms tightly against her chest and hung her head. 'It seems as if you're deliberately trying to upset me. I've got enough to cope with as it is.'

'No, I'm not! You just keep picking on me, and I can't do anything right. What am I supposed to have done anyway?'

His mother hesitated before answering.

'One, you've not been going to school. Two, you've been hanging about with that girl who's always in trouble, and three, you brought that animal into the house.'

'What animal? I don't know what you're talking about.'

'Don't tell lies, James! What is the matter with you?' Now she was shouting. 'You know I don't like cats, but there it was, strolling about on the lawn as if it owned the place.'

'Oh,' said James. 'That cat.'

'There, you see. You do know about it, don't you?'

'OK! But it just follows me around. I didn't bring it here to upset you!' Now he was shouting.

'Well, get rid of it! I won't have it here! Do you understand? I won't have it! James? Come back! Come back here right now!'

But James was fleeing from the house and his mother's angry voice. He didn't stop until he reached the promenade, flinging himself down on one of the seats. His face was burning. He clenched his fists and ground them into his temples. People were staring at him. He looked up and glared at them.

'What're you looking at? Seen enough, have you?'

The people turned away, shaking their heads. He threw an empty Coke can after them, but they didn't turn around. He made his way to the beach and walked towards the sea caves under the cliffs, kicking at anything in his way. The caves were a long way off, so he scrambled high on the rocks, which jutted out into the sea. His hands were bruised and sore, but he didn't care. All he wanted to do was to get away. He leaned back against the rock face and stared towards the sea. A seal's grey head appeared. It was close enough for him to see its whiskers. The tide was coming in.

A peculiar sound made him jump. He turned to see what it was. The man who called himself Michael was standing below him. He held two large stones, which he slowly rubbed together, making a harsh, grating noise. As James watched, he carefully placed them on the ground then bent and stared at them. Emma was right; the man was very strange. Michael looked up to where James was standing and pointed, showing him the pathway down. Then he stood motionless as if he himself were made of stone. James followed the pointing finger to the ground.

'Thanks.'

Michael began to walk towards the caves, indicating with a curt wave of his hand for James to follow. He was humming to himself. Every few steps, he stopped and moved a rock or small stone, then held his head to one side as if listening for something before nodding and moving on. He walked with dragging, sideways steps and partly bent knees. James looked towards the sea, wondering if the seal was still there. When he turned back, Michael was nowhere to be seen.

He stared towards the place where Michael had been standing wondering where he had gone. He was just about to walk away, when the air in front of him shimmered, like the silvery passage of a breeze on water. He blinked. The man was back. It must have been a trick of the light.

'I thought you'd gone.'

Michael smiled. 'Come,' his voice was almost a whisper.

Suddenly, they were walking into mist. James couldn't even see his feet. Just as he was becoming uneasy, it melted away. They were standing in the middle of a huge, stone circle. A sound like Michael's humming was all around them.

'What's making that noise?'

'The stones. It's the power in the stones. Put your hands on them and feel it. It's in them all. Watch.'

Michael stood in front of the tallest stone and slowly walked towards it. Then, without a moment's hesitation, he walked right into it and vanished. James ran to it. As he touched it, he could feel the energy surging through him.

'Where are you?' he called. 'Come back!'

'I'm here.'

The voice was behind him. James stared at the man in amazement. He was dressed in a shining, white robe. His handsome young face was very stern, and he carried a diamond-studded sword.

'Who are you?' James could hardly find his voice. 'What is this place?'

'I am the Keeper of the Stones, as you, James, are the Keeper of the Ancient Knowledge. I have something for you. Here. Take it.'

In his hand lay a small, carved stone. It was a dragon made of quartz. James picked it up. It felt warm to the touch.

'This is my gift to you. It will help to guide you and warn you of danger. You asked me where we are. This is the Place of Dreams, the place of all the forgotten magic. The stone circle represents the Earth and the ring of power that protects it. The rhythm of the earth is shifting out of balance. The power is weakening. Long ago, men were welcomed here, but now there are few for whom the gates will open. They will open for you, James. Now you must go. Find the Tower of the Weaver. She has every secret, every whispered word and thought caught up in her silken cloth, and she has been waiting for you.'

'But how will I find my way to the gates? What if I can't get back?'

'Then we are lost, James, truly lost. You must look for the place where light shifts through air like ice sparkling in sunlight. Where you will feel the tingle, like pins and needles in your fingers and a prickling on your face, as time slides past that space. Look, James. Do you see it?'

James nodded. He could feel it too. He pointed the stone dragon towards the gate. The carving began to glow with a warm, amber light as he walked into the mist.

Nothing had changed as he arrived back on the beach. The tide was no further up than when he'd left. He felt for the stone dragon and took it out of his pocket. It was now a deep violet in colour, and he could feel a slight vibration from it. He held it up to his ear and listened. The humming sound, though very faint, was there. He put it back in his pocket and started walking towards the town.

Emma found him in the amusement arcade.

'Where've you been? I've been looking all over for you. Went up to your house, but it sounded like your mum and dad were having words, so I came back down here.'

In a hushed voice, he told her all that had happened. He wanted to talk and talk. To blot out everything to do with home and everything else that was happening. He felt as if he were in a dark tunnel, which was getting smaller and blacker, pressing in on him, squeezing him out of existence.

'James. It's OK.'

He felt her hand on his arm as she led him out into the street.

'I hate them! Really, really hate them! I'm not going home. I'll run away like you. That'll teach them. And all that other stuff. It's just not true, any of it, is it?'

'I don't know, James,' she sighed. 'If I were you, I wouldn't run away. You've got a nice home and a mum and dad. I haven't. I wish I did.'

'Yeah. Right. So what anyway!'

'So what? You don't know nothin'. You're just a spoiled brat! You wouldn't survive a night out there all on your own!'

She stamped her foot on his toe and glared at him. 'Why am I even bothering?'

'So tell me then. What's the big deal?'

OK. I'll tell you what the big deal is. Ever had to find food in bins? Ever been hit and locked up in the dark? Well, have you?' She poked him hard on his arm. He flinched.

'Hey! That hurt!'

'Oh, what a shame! Softy! Mammy's boy!' Emma was so upset she was sobbing. She poked him again. 'Want to hear some more? Bet you've never thought someone was going to kill you—or worse!' Her face was flushed with anger, and she pressed, 'Have you?!'

He didn't know what to say and pushed his hands into his pockets.

His fingers touched the little talisman. Emma had started to run off up the street. He followed her.

'Emma! Wait! Come back!'

He caught up with her and grabbed her by the arm.

'I'm sorry, Em. Wanna talk about it?'

She shook her head. The stone dragon was warm in his hand.

'Emma, look what Michael gave me.'

As he dropped the carving into her upturned palm, the colour deepened to a dull red. She gasped holding it towards him.

'It's moving, James. Is it alive?'

'I'm not sure. I don't think so, not like we are anyway.'

She gave it back to him. 'What are you going to do?'

James shrugged. 'Dunno,' he said very quietly. 'I just don't know.'

DAISY

Daisy was crying. Her face was red and blotchy.

'Has she been touching that cat?' his mother asked.

James looked at his sister. 'Have you?'

'No! I didn't!'

Their mother shushed her. 'Well, you know, it could have fleas.'

'I'm sure it hasn't, Mum. He likes Daisy.'

'You can't trust cats James. Anyway, I thought I told you to chase it away. It was still mooching about here yesterday. I saw it in the garden and threw a stone at it.'

James stifled a grin.

'It's not funny.'

'No,' he said, looking out of the window to hide his amusement.

'This child has been crying half the night. I brought her downstairs in the end, but now she won't go back to her bedroom. Every time I take her in there, she screams. She keeps saying something about some little man. I can't understand it. I think we've got mice now as well.'

'Cats catch mice,' said James.

His mother ignored him. Daisy had stopped crying.

'I like mice,' she said. 'And Thomas. He's nice. Can I sleep in your room, James? Please? The nasty man won't come in there.'

'I think that's a good idea. Just for a couple of nights until she settles down.'

James shook his head.

'No way, Mum! She's such a pain! Daisy, don't be such a baby. I don't want her in my room. It's not fair!'

57

But his mother was determined.

'Now then. Let's not argue about this. It will be a great help at the moment because your dad has to go away for a while, and I have to go with him. I'm sorry, James. I meant to tell you earlier.'

She waited for James to respond, but he couldn't think of anything to say.

'I don't know how long we'll be away. Anyway, Aunt Caroline will be here shortly. She's been looking forward to taking care of you. Don't worry about the mice. I'll put some traps down before I go.'

James groaned. This was the end.

'Auntie Cei likes cats,' he said. 'And so do I. I don't see why I should chase it off when you're not going to be here, especially if I have to have *her* in my room!'

'All right! Just don't have it wandering all over the house, OK?'

He nodded. At least he wouldn't have to tell lies about that now.

'Don't worry about the mice. I'll see to them.'

His mother smiled and gave him a hug. He hugged her back.

'Will Dad get better, Mum?'

She didn't answer straight away and when she did her eyes were troubled.

'I hope so James. I'm sure he will, one of these days'.

Auntie Cei was a laugh but James wondered what she would think when she saw Daisy. He didn't have long to wait.

'This child is not right,' she said. 'I hope she's not coming down with something. She could you know.'

James nodded, not sure what to say. He wondered what Daisy had been saying about the little man and decided to have a look in her bedroom. The horrible smell was still there. He peered under the bed and behind the wardrobe but found nothing. Just as he was leaving, he caught a movement in the corner behind the door. It was a plump, grey mouse.

'Gotcha,' he breathed and went to grab it. The mouse scuttled off at lightning speed, disappearing behind the bed. As he pulled the bed away from the wall, he thought about what the cat had said.

'If you're what I think you are, come out now.'

A tiny head appeared, followed by another. He sat down on the floor in front of them.

'You took your time.'

James couldn't help but laugh.

'First that cat, now talking mice. What next?'

'We're glad you think it's funny.' They spoke together, looking from one to the other.

'We don't do we? It's not safe here, you know. We're lucky to be around, aren't we?'

James was still chuckling.

'That cat said you were calling yourselves spies.'

The mice nodded.

'Well, come on then. I like secrets.'

'He's not going to like this, is he? No.'

They both hung their shaking heads. The plumpest one cleared his throat.

'We know what's frightening Daisy, don't we? Yes. And they mean to hurt her too. We can't stay here now, can we? No. We can't.'

James was no longer amused.

'So. Tell me!'

The mice moved closer to him, and he remembered their names. They peered cautiously around them before they spoke.

'She's told you,' said Robbit. 'But you're not listening,' said Pest. 'No.'

They were talking together again.

'That nasty faerie man is very bad. His claws are long and sharp like thorns. He comes at night. Yes. He likes the dark to hide in. Then he sneaks in to steal her away. Yes.'

James felt sick.

'And the awful smell? It's him, isn't it?'

They nodded.

'Where is he now?'

'Near,' they said. 'Always near.'

Later that night, James woke with a start. He looked across to his sister's bed but he could hardly see her. The darkness seemed to be much deeper there. An ill-defined shape was beginning to form. As he watched, it thickened and started move. A couple of feet from the floor, two points of red light glowed like coals in the blackness. They looked like eyes. Two wicked red eyes, which were staring straight into his. Fear froze his mind. He couldn't look away. The foul smell was beginning to make him choke. He could hear a snuffling sound like an animal sniffing out its prey. Daisy whimpered in her sleep. The eyes turned towards her. Suddenly, a spitting fury hurled itself across the room as a blinding flash tore through the blackness, splitting it apart. Behind it, James could see a cave. The light, bursting with energy, blazed behind the fearsome presence driving it before it, chasing it away. Something wailed in the distance. James pulled the duvet tight around his head as sparks threatened to set fire to his hair.

'You can come out now. Mr Nasty's gone. No thanks to you.'

Thomas sat on the end of James's bed. His whiskers were singed.

'Was that you? It didn't look like you.'

'You don't say.'

The cat's eyes had narrowed to slits. 'See. I keep telling you I'm something else. Well, come on. Don't just sit there. We have to go. Just in case you haven't noticed, your sister's in big trouble.'

'What was that?'

'That James, was just a little "nasty". A minion of the very worst of them. Nothing I can't handle though.'

'Will she be safe if we get her away from here?'

Thomas stared up at him.

'You just don't get it, do you? She can't go anywhere now—it's too late for that. They're trying to steal her spirit. You know. The bit that makes you who you are. They won't kill her. No. Not yet. It's you they're after, so if you want to help her, you'd better wake up and start listening.'

The sight of the cat's brown whiskers was making James giggle. Even now, he was still finding it difficult to believe that this was real.

'Something funny, is there? Well, do tell—or is this some kind of private joke?'

James couldn't speak. As they made their way downstairs, Thomas caught sight of himself in the hall mirror. He stopped in his tracks, his fur standing on end as if he'd had an electric shock.

'Ow!' he yowled. 'This can't be me! This is too bad. My looks have been spoiled!'

As he stared at himself, bits of his frizzled whiskers began to drop off.

'Just look at me. I'm not fit to be seen.'

He yowled again as he made his way, muttering and spluttering, out of the house.

DRAGON

Auntie Caroline had introduced herself to Emma, invited her in, and was serving her tea and toast.

'Want some?'

James shook his head.

'Come along, James. You must eat something, mustn't he?'

'Nice,' Emma nodded, spreading another slice with peanut butter. 'Have some.'

Auntie Cei put a bowl of milk down in front of Thomas. He turned his nose up at it, and she laughed.

'How's that sister of yours this morning, James?'

'Not sure. Still asleep, I think.'

How could he tell his aunt what he had seen? What if he'd imagined it? But then there was the cat, and the mice. His appetite for breakfast quickly vanished.

'What're you two up to today then?'

'Dunno. Go down the beach or something.'

'An old friend of mine is coming over today. Be nice if you could meet her. She's called Jayne Fellows.'

James stood up, feeling decidedly uncomfortable again.

'You ready, Em?'

As they left the kitchen, he looked back at his aunt. She waved to him.

'Better see to Daisy,' he called. 'She won't wake up.' Then he ran before his aunt could question him.

They didn't stop until they got to the park. Emma was out of breath. Thomas appeared, as if from nowhere, and jumped up onto the wall beside them.

'New, are they?' James nodded towards the cat's shiny, black whiskers.

'Not a word, young man. Not a word.'

James grinned.

'OK. So what now?'

'You, James, are going to say hello to a dragon. Well, that's what it calls itself. You've met it before mind. It's grown a bit now, but it still doesn't look like any dragon I've ever seen. Bit of a joke really.'

The thought of more peculiar stuff happening wiped the grin from James's face.

'I thought we were supposed to find some Weaver person.'

'You are. All in good time James but first, you must talk to the dragon.'

James was beginning to feel sick again.

'And just how are we going to do that?'

The cat jumped down. 'Easy,' he said. 'Just follow me.'

James had to drag a protesting Emma through the gate. They landed on a hillside overlooking a rocky valley. Thomas led them down towards a short, plump man who looked vaguely familiar.

'This,' he said, 'is Mr Witty. Wouldn't blame you if you can't remember him. He's the most useless wizard you'll ever meet in your life.'

Mr Witty held out his hand, tripped over a stone, and landed in a heap at James' feet.

'See. Just like I said. Can't even get a handshake right. What a loser!'

James was trying to think where he'd seen the man before. Mr Witty was struggling to get up, and James moved forward to help him. A sharp shock stung his hand as he touched the wizard, making him jump.

'Ouch! What was that?'

'Oops. Dear me. I do apologise. Bit of static. Be with you in a moment.'

Mr Witty puffed and panted as he hauled himself up from his knees.

'Ever heard of a diet?'

The wizard ignored the cat and leaned on his staff, breathing heavily.

'Or starving? Perhaps a good boiling would do the trick. Mm? Well, maybe not. After all, we'd never find a pot big enough!'

'Stop it Thomas,' said Emma. 'You're making me laugh.'

The wizard glared at the cat, then said, 'It's very nice to see you again James, not like some I could mention. I believe Michael has given you a little gift. May I see it, do you think?'

'You mean this?' James showed him the carved dragon.

'Ah. Yes. That's it. The talisman. A very special thing. You must be sure to keep it safe.'

Thomas yawned loudly. 'Get on with it, will you? We don't want to be here all day.'

Mr Witty was becoming very cross.

'Just ignore him, vain creature that he is. I don't know why the Master puts up with him. Be silent, cat!'

A cough stopped the argument. Emma gasped and pointed towards a small cloud of smoke.

'That,' said Thomas, 'is your so-called dragon. Say hallo, everyone. Don't get too close though. Not a good idea. Like I said, there's no control. He just can't get the hang of it.'

The smoke cleared, and a dragon not much taller than James, was walking towards them. It was light grey in colour with short, orange horns and eyes of the palest blue.

'Quick! Get out of the way. If he sneezes, we're done for.'

Thomas was running backwards and forwards in front of them. 'Stay back, you fool!'

The dragon stopped and started to sniff.

'Oh. No! Here we go again. Don't you dare blow soot all over me!'

'Quiet!' Mr Witty shook his staff at Thomas, who shot up into the air and landed with a thump on the other side of the valley.

'Thank goodness for that. Now where were we?'

The dragon's head was very close to James. He put his hand up to touch it. Their eyes met, and something very strange happened. He could see both himself and the dragon at the same time. Somehow, he was inside the dragon's mind, but it was more than that. The dragon was also in his. They were like two pieces of a jigsaw fitting together to finish the puzzle.

Mr Witty was nodding and smiling.

'Good. Very good. Just as we'd hoped. Now then. Your minds may be joined, but you still need to learn how to speak to each other. Come, Emma. We must leave them. We can't help them now. They must work this out for themselves.'

James's hand was tingling more than when he had been holding the runes. He felt dizzy, and pain shot across his temples. The dragon leaned towards him, making a low, rumbling sound. As its head touched his, James felt power streaming through him. He could see it radiating from every rock, tree and stone. An immense circle of energy coursing through time, pulsing with the rhythm of the earth, and he knew that every living thing was connected. He could see huge caves of ice, the terrifying brilliance of fire storms radiating from the sun and the dazzling glare of the stars in the night. He was seeing dragons, aflame with light, blazing like comets across the skies. Words were starting to form in his mind. A great, booming voice made him jump back in alarm; holding his hands over his ears.

'Too loud,' he shouted. 'Turn down the volume!'

Smoke began to curl from the dragon's nose as he tried not to sneeze.

'Run!' shouted Thomas, but it was too late. A great shower of soot and sparks shot into the air. Then, as the dragon tried to blow them away, his breath fanned into flame. He spread his wings to shield James from the heat. The voice in James's head squeaked with delight.

'I can do it! Look at me. Look!'

At that moment James realised that this was Wisp, the tiny dragon he'd met in Mrs Fellows's cottage. He also knew that now he could breathe fire, he was beginning to grow up, and his lisp would be gone forever. The dragon blew again, and apart from a few sparks and a small fall of soot, he breathed fire.

'I've got it! I've got dragon fire!'

Wisp was stamping his feet in excitement. Thomas was not amused.

'Yeah. Yeah. So what took you so long? And what about me? Look what you've done to my nice, shiny coat. I just can't believe it. Well?'

The dragon hiccupped as he inspected the damage to the cat's fur. 'It doesn't look that bad to me. I can't see any difference really. Don't see why you have to make so much fuss. With your special skills, you could fix it in an instant.'

James grinned as he felt Wisp's amusement. Thomas walked away from them shaking his head. As James watched him, his thoughts turned to Daisy. The dragon felt his sadness.

'We must do something,' he whispered.

As Wisp agreed with him, images began to flood James's mind.

'This is the lore of dragons. It's the knowledge that links us and is shared by us all. But something has been hidden, even from us. We can feel our power weakening and are helpless to stop it. I can only show you what we already know.'

At first, James could see nothing. Then he heard the sound of weeping. An icy cold seeped into his mind, numbing his body. He began to shiver. He was rushing through a dark, treeless landscape. The air stank of dead things. He could smell burning. In the distance something was howling. The sound echoed, as if it were coming from the depths of a bottomless well. Lightning flashed above him, revealing the unthinkable. He closed his eyes, trying to blot it out, as the worst of all nightmares came rushing towards him, reaching out to drag him down towards its monstrous, gaping mouth. He screamed in terror. The thing was nearly on him. He could smell its rotten breath as he felt himself falling. The scream froze on his lips, and he collapsed unconscious to the ground, unable to cope with the shock of what he'd seen. But the dragon had seen it too.

THE HOUSE OF SECRETS

James woke up on the sofa in Mr Fairweather's house. Emma was leaning over him, looking very worried. He tried to sit up, but his head hurt too much.

'Ah. Here you are. Well done, my boy. Well done indeed.' Mr Fairweather patted him on the shoulder. 'Headache? No problem. This'll cure it.'

James took the glass of dark brown, goey-looking liquid. It smelled like a vile mix of garlic, onions, and over-boiled sprouts.

'I'm not drinking this. It's disgusting!'

'Now, now, James. Be brave. Take your medicine like a man.'

Go on, Jamie. Don't be a baby.'

Emma was grinning. Mr Fairweather stood next to her, twiddling his thumbs. James held his nose and swallowed the foul-smelling stuff as fast as he could.

'Ugh!' he said. 'Don't ever ask me to do that again!' The headache was gone.

'You've had a very narrow escape, James. You and that dragon are going to have to sort this out. That abomination nearly had you both. Two for the price of one, so to speak. You must never get that close again.'

James shuddered as he remembered what he'd seen. The voice of the dragon whispered in his mind. 'So sorry, James. But now at last we know the one we seek.'

James could feel the dragon's sadness. *I'm OK. Really*, he thought. *You didn't know that would happen.*

'Is your name really Wisp?' James asked him.

Mr Fairweather was stroking Thomas, who was sitting on the table. The cat was purring loudly.

'For now,' the dragon answered. 'One day I will be given another name, but I don't know when that will be.'

As James watched, he realised that Mr Fairweather looked a bit like Mr Witty. He even sounded like him. 'Do you know any wizards?' he asked.

'He certainly does. It's him. Of course there's a bit of a difference in the weight department, but it's him all right. He's a Seer in this world and a wizard in that. Not much good at either if you ask me,' Thomas answered.

Mr Fairweather dismissed the cat with a wave of his hand.

'Just ignore him, James. I believe Michael thinks you should find the Weaver.'

'Yes,' said Emma. 'And some old tower as well.'

'Ah. Yes. Now where is she likely to be these days, I wonder? Has a habit of moving around, you know. She and the tower, that is. Let me have a think. Where's that owl? He'll know. Just the kind of a place for an owl to hang out. I'll give him a call.'

Mr Fairweather rummaged in several drawers before he found what he was looking for. Pencils, bits of string, sweets and stale cake, buttons, beads, corks, and Christmas candles overflowed from the drawers and fell to the floor.

'Got it. I knew it was here somewhere.'

He put a small tin whistle to his lips and blew. Three wine glasses fell off a shelf and shattered before they hit the ground. Thomas jumped from the table and ran for the door.

'I keep forgetting it does that. Oh well. Never mind. Ah. Here he is.'

A big, brown owl swooped in through the window and landed on top of the TV.

Mr Fairweather turned to James and Emma. 'Cranlow is a very helpful owl so I'm sure he won't mind assisting you to find the Weaver and her tower.'

'The Weaver?' Cranlow's voice was even more hooty than usual. 'You won't get far with her. She doesn't like visitors. I wouldn't bother if I were you.'

'Well, you aren't, and we have to speak to her. Do you know where she is or not?'

'Well, well. A disrespectful boy.'

Emma stepped in front of James.

'Please, Mr Owl. It's just that we're all a bit upset. He didn't mean to be cheeky, did you James? Please say you'll help us.'

'Hm. I may have to give it some thought.'

Cranlow looked at James, who was shaking his head.

'Well, I suppose I must. The Master said I had to help, especially as it's so important.'

Mr Fairweather clapped his hands to get their attention.

'Good. Come along then. No time to waste. Off you go with Cranlow.'

'What now?' hooted the owl. 'I've only just arrived.'

'Yes. Yes. Can't be helped. Off you go. No choice in the matter. We'll dance for you, James. It might help. Hope so. Anyway, good luck. Oh, just a quick tip to help you get back: listen for the sound of bells.'

They followed the speeding owl across town, racing to keep up with him. He turned into the driveway of a neglected old house not far away from the Council tip. The garden was overgrown with weeds. Brambles and stinging nettles choked everything, growing through the rubbish thrown onto what had once been a lawn.

'Here we are,' said Cranlow. 'Welcome to the House of Secrets.'

'What, this dump?' said Emma. 'You can't be serious.'

The owl peered down his beak at her.

'Suit yourself. It's not my problem.'

The windows were cracked and crusted with dirt. Ivy covered the walls and pushed its way through the rotted windowsills into the darkened rooms. Faded, green paint peeled off the front door. It opened surprisingly easily, and they found themselves in a dingy hallway. Old newspapers, broken pots, bits of stick and fallen leaves littered the floor. Grubby cobwebs, full of the husks of dead insects and other unmentionable things, hung from the ceiling. The door slammed shut behind them, making Emma jump.

'I think I want to go home,' she said in a very small voice.

'Too late.' Cranlow was hovering in front of them. 'No turning back now. Follow me and keep up. Don't go wandering off. Never know what you might meet in here.'

They fought their way through the clinging webs as they hurried after the owl. At the top of a flight of very steep and creaky stairs, they lost sight of him. They rushed along the corridor in front of them, trying to catch up, but he had gone. They stood still and shouted his name as loud as they could, but their voices just echoed back at them.

Without Cranlow, they were lost.

'We could go back the way we came,' Emma suggested. 'That should get us out of here.'

James shook his head. He was beginning to feel very scared.

'Which way is that, Emma? Everywhere looks the same to me.'

'Footsteps,' she said. 'We can follow our footsteps in the dust.'

They turned, but as they watched, their footsteps lifted from the floor and danced in front of them before falling apart in the air. The footsteps were gone as if they'd never been there at all. There was no way back.

The corridor behind them was shrinking. It was getting shorter and narrower. The floor began to tilt, and a great booming sound, worse than thunder, nearly deafened them. They turned to run, but their way was barred by an immense, iron-studded, door, which filled the corridor and was higher than the eye could see. The booming noise was getting worse. All around them, the dust was beginning to move, stirring and drifting, coiling and lifting, shaping itself into spooky, white phantoms. James suddenly realised he was holding the little stone carving. As he took it out of his pocket, it shone with a cold, blue light. The ghostly shapes were getting closer. Emma was squeezing his arm so hard that it hurt. The blue light became brighter, spreading out in every direction, keeping the creepy ghosts away. He stared at the door, realising he could see right through it. He was seeing with the eyes of the dragon. Emma was too frightened to move. He shook her hand free of his arm.

'That's the way,' he called out, pointing to the door. 'You've got to trust me, Em. Just close your eyes and run!'

THE TOWER OF THE WEAVER

The ghosts were gone. They were standing in a small courtyard next to a stone tower. Cranlow was perched on the branch of a gnarled tree, which was growing out of the wall.

'It won't do, you two. I thought I told you to keep up. Not too much to ask was it?'

He sounded more haughty than ever

'You went too fast,' said Emma. 'It was horrible. Things were trying to get us.'

'Get you? Oh dear. What a to-do.'

The owl's eyes were closing as he spoke. He started to snore.

'Cranlow!' James shouted. 'Wake up!'

The owl nearly jumped out of his feathers.

'Wake up. Wake up. Who? No need to shout. I could have had a turn, you know. Then where would you be? And that wouldn't do, would it, for you? What a cross boy you are.'

'Don't blame me! First you get us lost and clear off without us. Then when we find you, you go to sleep. What sort of help is that?'

Cranlow produced a pair of gold rimmed spectacles from under his right wing and made a big show of placing them onto his beak.

'Keep you awake, will they?' James was losing patience fast.

'Do remind me, will you, of why you are here. I think I've forgotten. Perhaps another little nap will help me to remember.'

'Oh. Please, Mr Owl. He didn't mean it and he's very sorry aren't you, James?' Emma pleaded.

James scowled at her but kept quiet.

'His sister, Daisy is in trouble. Bad stuff is happening, and it's getting worse. That's why we have to find the Weaver.'

Cranlow's eyes were closed tight. James paced up and down in despair.

'Emma, this is hopeless. He's just a waste of space.'

The owl's eyes opened very slowly.

'I shall ignore that remark. Come closer. I need to look at you. Make sure you haven't brought any unwelcome travellers along with you. Can't be too careful these days.'

As Cranlow's silent wings closed over James's head, he could smell the night. The owl's feathers were as soft as thistledown.

'Nothing yet. They're close though. It's the power of the dragon that keeps them away.'

'So how do we find this Weaver woman then?'

'You've already found her, James. She's here. Up there.'

James looked up at a small window almost at the top of the tower and groaned.

'All those steps,' said Emma.

'No. No.' Cranlow hovered in front of them. 'Nothing is as it seems in this place. Well. What are you waiting for?'

As they entered the tower, the walls closed behind them. They waited in silence, watching what looked like petals floating in the air all around them.

'Oh,' said Emma, holding out her hands. 'They're butterflies. There must be thousands of them. They're catching that sparkling stuff on their wings. The air's full of it.'

'It's all over you too Em. And me. I wonder where it's coming from.'

The butterflies were all around them, flying in a great spiral. James and Emma felt themselves being lifted up and up, drifting through jewelled light towards the Weaver. They landed on a wooden platform just behind her. As she turned her veiled face towards them, the butterflies dropped gently back amongst the glittering motes of silk. The lustrous colours of her robe glistened as she moved. A great loom stretched out before her, and from it fell the shimmering dust that painted the butterflies' wings. Her voice was gentle and sounded like the tinkling of a crystal bell.

'This loom weaves dreams and secrets. The hopes and fears of all the world are woven into its silken threads. Come closer to me, James. I have been waiting for you here. So many years have come and gone. If you succeed, I shall at last be free to join my people once again. Bring me the talisman that I may look into your destiny.'

James moved slowly towards her, with Emma so close behind she was tripping over his heels. The stone seemed to have lost its magic. As he held it out to her, the eyes of the dragon revealed the face behind the Weaver's veil. He knew her name. Seremela, a sylph and winged spirit of the air, held captive to the loom until the earth was safe again. The golden chain, which held her fast, clasped tightly around her tiny waist. The harshness of her task showed in the deeply etched lines around her eyes and mouth. Her once bright-turquoise hair was streaked with grey. The talisman began to glow between her hands.

'Sleep, James,' she said. 'And dream so I can see the secret that you keep.'

James could hear a voice calling his name. The voice became louder. It was Emma as she shook him awake. The Sylph leaned towards him and held his face in her careworn hands.

'I have seen the unspeakable, that most dreadful and merciless monster of them all. It is reaching out for you. Its vicious menace creeps ever closer. Its touch is the curse of living death. But I will show you what you seek, even though it will be but a poor reflection. This is the very core of life itself, the source of all the power on earth and far beyond. The great circle, created by the gods and held in place by dragons. Sadly, I cannot tell you where to look. That secret place is hidden, even from me. Look.'

At the touch of the Weaver's hand, the loom hummed into life, weaving the silken threads into a vibrant cone of dazzling brilliance, which filled the tower. As it spiralled and spun, the brightness intensified, becoming too much for human eyes to bear.

'When you find this, the end will be very near. Even now the core is weakening, the light has dimmed. The dragon must fulfil his destiny and take his place within the circle. You must help him, James. And you must find the Old One where he sleeps, suspended in time in his crystal bubble, and wake him. Only then can the dragon take his name. The name he must be given freely, as a gift, even though the one who gives it knows it will mean that his life will be over.'

She smiled at James, feeling his fear, and her heart was filled with sadness.

'I will be with you, James, to ease your way. Now you must go and leave me here to wait and hope that all will turn out well.'

Thomas hurried towards them as they arrived back in the courtyard.

'What took you? Get lost in there or something? Not surprised with that overstuffed bird in charge. Now if you'd had me . . .'

'Well, we didn't,' said Emma. 'You'd cleared off. I saw you sneaking out when Mr Fairweather blew that whistle.'

'I was thinking about my hearing. It's very sensitive, you know. I can't have the likes of him taking liberties with it.'

'Is there any point in your being here?' James scowled at the cat, who pretended to swat an imaginary fly. 'Because, if you haven't got anything useful to say you might as well just go away.'

'Right. That's fine by me. Well, cheerio then. I'll just have myself a really nice day, while you go off all by yourselves.'

Thomas inspected his claws, rearranged his whiskers, yawned very loudly, and vanished.

Emma groaned. 'What now, James? We need him.'

'Yeah. Like a hole in the head. Oi! Cat! Come back!'

The House of Secrets loomed over them, silent and ominous. James's voice echoed back at them from the rugged, granite walls. Shadows lengthened across the courtyard. It would be night soon. Brambles pulled at their clothes as they hunted for a way out. A creaking noise made them turn towards the house. A door had appeared and was slowly inching its way open. Something stirred within the gloom, as a dark shape began to move towards them. They backed away from it until they could go no further, huddling together against the ivy-covered walls. A puff of wind stirred the leaves around them. With it came the faintest sound of bells. Emma heard it first. She pulled at James, too scared to speak, as the shapeless mass wormed ever closer. In the corner, they saw a small archway, half concealed under the brambles and the ivy. The hideous, slithering shape was moving faster. They tried to run but an overwhelming sense of dread held them fast. The squelching mess was only feet away. For a fleeting moment, the sound of bells was all around them, breaking their paralysing fear. Slime oozed towards them as they fled, as fast as their legs would carry them, towards the archway and the bells.

They ran until they were exhausted. When they looked back, there was no sign of the house, the tower, or anything. Emma shuddered.

'Did that really happen? What was that thing?'

James shook his head. They heard the bells again and hurried towards the sound. As they got closer, they saw figures dancing inside a circle of stones.

'It's the Morris dancers, James. Old Mr Fairweather said to follow the sound of bells.'

As the dancers moved and swayed, they appeared to float above the ground. The ragged tatters of their coats rose and fell like multicoloured feathers in the air. The feathers of exotic birds, mysterious and dreamlike, bobbing and weaving amongst the stones. As they watched, the air around the dancers began to shift, blending all the colours, spreading them like oil spilled on water as they slowly faded away.

Just then, Thomas appeared in front of them.

'Well. Don't just stand there, we must go. So, come on. Can't hang around here all day.'

'Go? Go where? Where've you been anyway?'

The cat ignored James and walked towards the largest of the standing stones. He looked back at James and Emma before melting into it. Then, just as they were beginning to think he'd abandoned them, his head poked out from the middle of it.

'Here.' he said. 'I've been here. Where else would I be? Come and see for yourselves. Or are you too scared?'

As James touched the stone, the surface changed, dissolving like ice in warm water. It felt spongy and damp. Emma had her eyes screwed tightly shut. It was like walking through cold fog.

RETURNING HOME

They were in the middle of a wood. No one spoke. There was no wind. Nothing stirred. They looked around them, fearing what they might see. The silence was so deep they were afraid to speak. Even Thomas seemed to have lost his tongue. James felt the hairs on the back of his neck begin to prickle. A man was walking towards them through the trees. His head and face were hidden by the concealing cowl of a cloak as black as midnight. Power flowed from him, making the air around him crackle. When he spoke, his full, rich voice resonated all around them. As Kallen Lupus summoned them towards him, an owl landed on his shoulder. It was Cranlow. Thomas wailed and spat, his eyes glinting with fury.

'What's he doing here? The last time I saw him, he was snoring loud enough to wake the black dragon himself!'

The wizard's expression was stern as he spoke to the cat.

'Now, Thomas. Let's not speak of the unspeakable. We don't want to invoke that just yet, do we?'

'Besides, you will need Cranlow to guide you through some of the more tricky bits. He can see through magic, remember, even when you can't. I have every faith in him. I'm sure he won't let you down, will you, Cranlow?'

The owl stared at each of them in turn, before shaking his head, and flying off again.

'Good. That's settled then. But first, you must go home. You need to see your family James, and Daisy has been asking for you. Your Aunt and Mrs Fellows have been looking after her well.'

'Can't you come with us, Master?' asked Thomas.

'I wish I could, but you must journey without me. I am needed elsewhere. Use the talisman to help you find your way. Beware of trickery, James. Your sister is safe as yet, but her fate is in your hands. You must have trust in each other until we meet again.'

James and Emma hung back. Emma sat on the ground with her head in her hands.

'But how will we know where to go?' she asked anxiously.

'Mrs Fellows and Mr Fairweather will help, and the Dancers will seek out the direction you must take,' the Master replied.

James turned to speak to the wizard, but he had already gone. Thomas stared up at Emma and twitched his whiskers willing her to get up.

'Come on, Emma. Just follow me. I know the way to James's house. It's not far and they're expecting us anyway.'

Thomas led them through the darkening wood until they saw the warm lights of Oakwood twinkling a welcome through the trees. They were all safely home. All except Cranlow, who was nowhere to be seen. As they walked through the door, Daisy came running to meet them.

'We've got pizza,' she said. 'And cake and strawberries.'

Auntie Caroline hugged them both. There were tears in her eyes, and she turned away quickly. Mrs Fellows smiled at James before asking Thomas to follow her into the hall.

'How's Dad?' James asked turning to his aunt. 'And where's Mum?'

'He won't be coming home for a while yet,' she replied. 'But he isn't any worse. Your mum is staying with him for the time being. She's fine and sends you her love.'

'And what about this, little one?' asked Emma as she piled more cake on to Daisy's plate.

'Under control, as you can see,' said Mrs Fellows as she came back into the kitchen. 'We keep a close watch and have our own special guardian to help.'

James was having difficulty keeping his eyes open and was falling asleep where he sat. Auntie Cei hugged him again.

'To bed, young man. You too, Emma. We'll talk tomorrow. Everything can wait until then.'

As James slept he dreamed, unaware of the cat who lay beside him watching him intently. The dream became deeper, touching the myth of the ancient past. A past where magic was strong and held all things in place. Shadows began to form, revealing a twilight beyond the reach of time.

The cat's shape was changing, blending with the shadows, his smoky silhouette weaving soundlessly through them. The shadow shapes were the spirits of beings long dead. Thomas moved quickly, probing ever deeper to find the one he sought. The one whom he knew would not want to be found. He had been present at its death and carried its spirit into a land far beyond the furthermost star. A land known only to the dead.

The spirit saw him and sped away, but not fast enough as the cat's dark form curled around it, holding it fast. The spirit stilled its flight and spoke the cat's true name.

'You have disturbed me, Evarin Dax. There will be a price to pay this time.'

Its voice rose and fell like echoes carried on the wind. Thomas tightened his grip as he replied, 'I think not, but you may redeem yourself yet. You know what I seek and will disclose it to me now! Even you cannot hide forever. And remember this, I know your name also, and when I speak it, you will reveal yourself and obey.'

The spirit struggled to break free.

'You think you can command me? There is not one of your kind who is strong enough to do that.'

'Oh, really?' Thomas released his hold ever so slightly. 'I think you'll find I can and I will, or would you prefer to answer to the Old One? The one who gave me my names and made me what I am. So, what do you say to that?'

There was no reply. Thomas knew he'd won for now. The spirit spoke again, his voice quieter than a whisper.

'The place you seek is not what you think. The Old One cannot be found there. The Fortress of the Moon is but a pathway through time and is no longer in the outer sphere of the world. Ask Kallen Lupus—he may be able to see through the wards that hide it, but I think not. Even so, the way is hazardous and unclear.'

'But this cannot be. We have to find the Old One and his guardian, or the forces of the dark will have us all. You are the only one who can enter the hidden places, places closed even to me, so you must have some idea where he is.'

Thomas was becoming very concerned. If the spirit didn't know, they were in real trouble.

'I can only tell you that you must pass through the Fortress of the Moon first. The boy James might be able to find the way with the help of the dragon. That is all I know, so you may now go and leave me in peace. I will not be disturbed by such as you again.'

Thomas watched as the dark angel shrank away, melting into the shadow shapes until he was gone.

'That's what you think,' he muttered as he made his way back to the sleeping James. 'The time is soon coming for you to make amends.'

Emma was very quiet at breakfast. James still hadn't appeared. She had woken in the early hours and was sure she'd seen a strange creature standing beside her bed. It had long silver hair and was wearing a bright-blue hat. She'd tried to sit up, but it had held out its hands and blown through them. The last she remembered were silvery sparkles drifting across her eyes. She sighed. Mrs Fellows sat in the chair opposite.

'You're looking very puzzled, young lady.'

'Yes. Well, I thought I saw something in my room last night. It wasn't scary or anything like that. I think it was just a dream, really.'

Mrs Fellows smiled.

'A bit scruffy looking with a blue hat?'

Emma nodded.

'That was Kob of the Blue. He's quite a one-off, you know. Part brownie and part elf. Extremely rare. He has very remarkable magic too. That's why he's here. To help to protect Daisy and look after the house. He's descended from the most ancient and noble line of elves. They are said to have come from a place far beyond the midnight sky. Their eyes are the colour of that sky and mirror the light of those distant stars. He loves apricot jam and peanut butter sandwiches with toasted marshmallows and chocolate cake. He's more elf than brownie, but he can still be easily upset sometimes. Best to leave him to us. We know the ways of his kind, and we certainly don't want to lose him. Ah. Here's Master James. How are you feeling, young man?'

James yawned then grinned. 'Still a bit tired but much better now, thank you.'

'Good, because I have someone here I'd like you to meet.'

Mrs Fellows clapped her hands twice. Then twice more. There was a creaking sound as the door of the china cupboard began to open. A spindly, brown leg appeared, slowly followed by another.

'Come along. Come along.' Mrs Fellows clapped her hands again.

The cupboard door opened a little wider as the creature finally dragged himself out.

'Well done. So glad you could make it.'

The creature scowled at Mrs Fellows, who smiled broadly at him.

'This,' she said, turning to James and Emma, 'is Kob.'

'I saw you,' said Emma. 'It was you, wasn't it? You blew silver sparkles on my eyes.'

Kob stared at Emma. He was as tall as a child of about eight or nine and very thin. His eyes matched the bright blue of his cap, and his hair shone in the light. He wore a shapeless brown tunic, which reached to his knees, that had two large pockets sewn onto the front of it, and a faded, grey cloak with a black hood. His shoes were the colour of a muddy puddle and looked like wooden clogs, but made no sound as he walked. A plaited belt, woven from straw, gathered the tunic about his waist. From it hung a silver whistle and a small, golden flute.

'Sleep is good,' he said.

'What are you?' asked James.

'I am what I am,' he replied. 'And so I am here.'

James pointed to the whistle. 'Can I blow it?'

'It brings and it sends it away. Here. It will not obey you.'

James took the whistle and blew. Nothing happened, so he tried again. An enormous spider with fierce, staring eyes materialised in the middle of the room right in front of him. Emma screamed. Kob snatched the whistle from James just as the spider was about to leap towards him. He tapped his feet as if beginning to dance, turned around three times, then put it to his lips. The spider stopped in mid-air. And then it was gone.

'What was that?' asked Emma as she crawled out from under the table. 'Where did it come from?'

Kob nodded towards James.

'She is Schlema. A queen. Not bad. Will help. He thought her. She came. Must learn though or much trouble. Kob will teach his young master, then he will know.'

They all turned as Kallen Lupus entered the room, closely followed by Thomas.

'Playing games, I see. Well now, James, you must listen to Kob, but first we must visit the Waters of Truth to set you on your way, and where I will explain the meaning of each of those symbols carved on the doors.'

The wizard pointed his staff towards the hallway, where a set of moss-covered stone steps opened up in the floor, leading to a dimly lit corridor. They followed the wizard in silence until they rounded yet another bend and the entrance to the Place of Knowing was in front of them. He beckoned to James, tapping each symbol in turn.

'You will need to remember every one of these. The Owl you already know. The Raven is a bird of great wisdom. You would be wise to listen to him. His name is Kark. Use the Mirror to seek the true image of those who may try to trick you. The Drum will herald your coming when you find the sleeping place of the Old One. It will hear you long before you hear it. The Dragon, the oldest and mightiest of his kind, will only assist you when Wisp stands before him in the Cave of The Winds. The Flute, magical and dangerous, is the one Kob will teach you to use. Now come, we lose time standing here.'

The chamber was cold. Emma was shivering as they approached the huge scrying bowl. The surface of the water was frozen. As the wizard laid both his hands flat against it, the ice began to change, becoming clear like glass.

'The place you seek is not here. We cannot see it. We are too far away.'

The sound tinkled around them like the jingle of tiny bells. Figures appeared beneath the ice. They were dancing. Threads spread out beneath the dancer's feet. Bright lines of light reflecting the energy of the earth, drew the dancers forward. The wizard withdrew his hands.

'Well, that's a start, I suppose, but we will learn no more here.'

They followed as he led them out of the chamber.

'Time for your lessons, James. You must go and find your teacher.'

Kob was waiting for him in the garden shed.

'Better here,' he said, peering closely at James. 'You will do this now?'

James nodded, feeling a little foolish.

'How does it work? The Master said it was dangerous.'

Kob handed James the silver whistle.

'You think, it will bring. Then you send away. You be strong. Not fear. Keep control. It be tricky. You learn, then you be safe. You start now.'

James groaned.

'You begin!'

Kob stamped his foot as James hesitated before putting the whistle to his lips. This time, he was careful as he tried to think of something nice. A picture of his favourite pudding entered his mind. Sticky toffee pudding with fudge sauce appeared in front of him. Kob nodded and clapped his hands.

'Now it must go. Now!'

The harder James tried, more and more appeared until they were surrounded by rapidly increasing mounds of pudding. He stopped.

'I can't do it.'

'You must!'

James was getting cross.

'You'll have to help me.'

Kob held out his hands.

'You must think it gone. Gone is what you must think.'

James tried again, this time making his mind blank as he blew. The pile of puddings disappeared.

Kob handed him the golden flute.

'This be more tricky. You will learn.'

As James took it, the two small heads of Robbit and Pest, popped out of the pockets in Kob's tunic.

'Hallo,' they said. 'Go on, James. You can do it.'

The flute felt warm in James's hands.

'I'm not doing any more before you tell me how it works.'

He held it out towards Kob, who put his hands behind his back.

'I will tell,' he said. 'Yes. All things be the same. All things be different. Magic can see. Magic can tell.'

James felt as if he were beginning to lose the plot. He sighed. Kob began to sing. The singing became louder and louder until James could no longer hear it as all the pots and tools lifted up from the shelves and hung, motionless in the air. Kob pointed to them, and they moved at his bidding. He stopped, and they all went back to where they belonged.

'There be a tune to all things. All things will dance to their tune. The pipe will know. The pipe will find. You must let it. You seek, you find, you know. You try.'

Kob walked out, leaving James holding a silver whistle and a golden flute and feeling very nervous indeed. He felt a tug at his trousers and looked down to find Robbit and Pest at his feet.

'Find our tune. We don't mind, do we? No.'

James shook his head.

'What if it goes wrong? What if I send you somewhere awful?'

The mice looked at each other, then Robbit said, 'Maybe. Maybe not.'

Then they both said together, 'Kob will come. Kob will know.'

They bowed, first to each other then to James as he lifted the flute to his lips.

'Well, OK then. Here goes.'

As James began to blow, he somehow knew to close his eyes. An image of the mice appeared in his mind. He blew gently as he began to hear the melodious sound of a singing harp, and he realised he was hearing their tune. He opened his eyes. The mice were gone. The flute felt hot. It was moving in his hands. He tried to drop it but couldn't let go. Panic filled him as the flute drew his hands up to his face and touched itself to his lips. The mice tumbled across the floor in front of him, but the tune went on, becoming ear piercingly loud, increasing in strength until it hurt. Just as he could bear it no longer, Kob touched his hands and began to chant. The deafening volume of sound stopped. James dropped to the floor in exhaustion. Kob knelt in front of him.

'This no good,' he said, helping James to sit up. 'Pipe control you. No good.'

James felt tears spill from his eyes, and he wiped them away with the back of his hand.

'You brave, young master. Try hard. Need help now. Kob help but need more. Must show dragon too. Give Kob magic stone. Will call dragon and teach while you sleep.'

For a moment James didn't know what Kob was asking for. He suddenly realised what he wanted and rummaged around in his pockets to find it. The talisman turned from violet to purple as he dropped it into Kob's outstretched hand.

'Go now. You tired. Sleep. We speak next day.'

It was dark as James left the shed and made his way to the house, closely followed by the two mice. Too tired even to eat his tea, he fell into bed and was asleep almost immediately.

He woke to find Kob leaning over him.

'You be safe now. Pipe know your tune. Will obey. Only use if things very bad. Whistle better for you. Dragon knows. Kob speak with him now too.'

He placed the talisman on the pillow next to James's still-sleepy head as Thomas jumped onto the bed.

'Come on! It's time we were leaving. Mr Fairweather and the dancers will be waiting for us in the park and they won't be very pleased if we're late.'

Kob placed his hand on James's shoulder. He looked sad.

'The way be hard. Not to trust strangers. Trouble come with many faces.'

He clapped his hands, and Robbit and Pest poked their heads out of his pocket.

'Be safe, young master,' he said as they left. 'I be thinking of you.'

'And us too,' called the mice. 'And us too.'

Later, after making their farewells, James and Emma stood quietly watching as the dancers trod in the footsteps of the ancestors, powerful beings of mystery and light, awakening the earth magic as they traced the hidden lines of their destiny.

The dancers moved as one, swaying and turning as the rhythm increased. Their colours mixed and merged, drawing them inwards and upwards, forming a multifaceted spiral like the butterflies at the Weaver's loom. Then, as quickly as it had formed, it collapsed. Standing in its place was Mr Fairweather.

'Where's that owl?' asked Emma. 'He's gone again.'

'Not too far away.' The Seer was walking towards them. 'He'll be here when we need him. No need to worry.'

Neither James nor Emma were very convinced.

'Ah. Here he is now.'

As Cranlow approached, they noticed a trail of colours, like those reflected in party bubbles, drifting behind him. Mr Fairweather said something under his breath and flapped his arms as the owl flew towards him.

'Can't have that. It's not Halloween. Owls aren't meant to glow in the light of day, especially this one. Too easy to trace by far.'

Cranlow didn't seem to be listening. The Seer turned to James.

'You need to follow Cranlow. The colours you saw just now are a reflection of the secret pathways only he can see.'

'What if he goes off and leaves us again like he's done before?' asked Emma. 'What will we do then?'

'He won't, will you, owl? He needs you just as much as you need him.'

As he spoke, he handed James a small rucksack.

'Just a small token to help you on your way. Things to eat and help to keep you well. Now then. Off you go. No point in hanging around here, is there?'

James took the pack and handed it to Emma. He already had one filled with food and drink from Auntie Cei and Mrs Fellows. Cranlow took off, flying in a large circle before calling to them to follow. It wasn't long before they realised he was heading towards the House of Secrets. James stopped, and Emma bumped into him before dropping to the ground as distress overcame her.

'I can't go back in there, not for anything. It's creepy and horrible. It frightens me like being shut up in the dark with no way of getting out. I can't do it, James. I just can't.'

'Well, you can't stay here either, can you?' hooted Cranlow.

Thomas stared up at Emma. Her eyes were troubled and brimming with tears.

'No, Emma. You can't stay here. You have to come with us. Besides, it's not all bad in there. Remember, you've got me to protect you. I'm not just any old cat, am I? Come on. Trust me. We'll be fine.'

James winced with embarrassment before pulling Emma to her feet. Through the mind of the dragon he'd glimpsed something of what they faced, and he was very afraid.

BACK TO THE HOUSE
OF SECRETS

The House was silent. They stood in a large hallway. There was no sign of the owl.

'Drat that overstuffed bird. I knew we'd have trouble with him.'

Thomas paced up and down in front of them.

'Use the talisman, James. I don't think we should just wait for him to show up.'

Emma pointed down the corridor that led away from the hallway. 'This looks like the only way to me.'

Thomas stopped pacing. 'Don't be so sure, young lady. Anything can happen in this house, as you already know.'

As James walked slowly around the hallway, the talisman began to glow and hum until he reached a point where the heat from the carved stone was almost burning his hand.

'This can't be right. There's nothing here. Just that wall.'

'Is it?' asked Thomas. 'Try again.'

James still couldn't see anything. The eyes of the dragon had deserted him. Emma tugged at his arm.

'Do something,' she said in a very low voice. 'You know that corridor? Well, it's gone, and that's not all. Does that wall seem closer than before?'

The hall was getting smaller by the minute, collapsing on itself like a pack of cards. The talisman had turned the zingy, gold of lemons. The colour streamed through James's fingers, making his hand glow red, as it flared, like a laser, against the approaching wall. They had no choice but to trust it. Thomas followed them through as the wall opened up before them.

The first thing they saw was Cranlow, perched on a pile of musty papers in the middle of a room stacked from floor to ceiling with mouldy old books. A fine dust rose up in a cloud as their feet disturbed it, sticking to their clothes and making them sneeze.

'Is this what you call helping? What kind of guide is it that doesn't bother to show up? Now then. Let me see. Useless, stupid, moth-eaten, way past your sell-by date? Shall I go on? No? Well perhaps not. Don't want to keep you awake now, do we?'

Cranlow puffed up his feathers.

'I can't do everything you know. The Master said I only needed to help with the tricky bits, remember? Cranlow this and Cranlow that. First the Master, now you, and there's that other Mr Witty nit too witty. All that, as well as being the highly respected guardian of the Great Book of Spells.'

'And we can all see how well you look after that, can't we?'

The cat was in his element.

Cranlow was about to respond when a large cobweb dropped from the ceiling and landed on his head. The more he tried to shake it off, the more it stuck to him. James was laughing so much he nearly fell over. Cranlow, who by now looked like a tasty morsel for a giant spider, bumped and rolled down the pile of papers towards them. They caught him before he reached the floor.

'OK.' said James. 'We'll free you but only if you promise never to go off and leave us again. Deal?'

'Oh dear. What to do? Really? No choice, have I?'

The owl paused, considered his feet, which were now pointing skywards, and finally muttered the word: 'Deal.'

After much fussing and phaffing, Cranlow eventually managed to remember the formula with which to command the Great Book of Spells. As it floated above them, he tapped its leather-bound cover three times with his beak. With a sound like the clapping of a thousand hands, the book became so small they could hardly see it. The owl caught it, tucked it up under his feathers, rearranged his spectacles, and said, 'Right. Are we ready then? I think you'll find we have to go this way.'

A flight of worn, stone steps led from the room into a narrow passageway. Spluttering candles dripped wax down the walls. As they passed by, the candles went out. No one dared to look back as they continued along the seemingly endless corridor. Thomas was becoming anxious and motioned James and Emma to move more swiftly, after peering into the darkness behind them. The white patch on his shoulder seemed to be getting bigger.

James could sense what the cat had seen. His legs felt tired and heavy. He closed his hand around the talisman, which was slowly turning to the darkest red.

Cranlow swooped around their heads before leading them up a flight of rickety wooden stairs into a short, oblong room. Mirrors covered the walls on either side of them. On one side, the mirrors reflected them in light, except for Thomas, who showed no image in the glass. The surface of the mirrors rippled like water as their reflections were caught in them. They felt drawn towards them, like sleepers in a dream. As they watched, the images in the glass behind them began to move and change. A dark shape was beginning to form. Huge, ebony black wings, furled outwards, blotting out the light, as the mirror curved stealthily towards them. Emma's attention was broken by the cat, hissing and spitting with fury. She shook James, with no effect.

'What's wrong with him? He won't move!'

She shook him again. Thomas's form was changing, becoming larger and stronger like that of a leopard. James pushed Emma away. His eyes were like a dead rabbit's.

'Look at him, Thomas. Look at his eyes!'

'They're calling him, Emma. They're calling him into the darkness.'

Cranlow hovered low over James's head, ready to pounce as Thomas sprang at him, knocking him forward, barking and snarling. The shock was enough to lift the disabling spell and with Emma pulling, and Cranlow holding onto his collar, they managed to drag James away. As they left the room, they heard a blood-curdling scream.

DARK MAGIC RISES

They were back in the wood. The House of Secrets was nowhere to be seen. Thomas was watching Cranlow as he flew towards them.

'Well now. Here he is again. So how do you rate your progress up to now then, owl? Nothing to say? What a surprise.'

The owl didn't seem to be listening.

Having a bit of a sulk are we?' Nearly finished us off, and you've got nothing to say?'

Cranlow mumbled something, as he landed on the branch of a nearby tree.

'What was that you said? If it was an apology you'd better speak up as I'm sure we'd all like to hear it.'

Emma was trying to talk to James. He was sitting, slouched on the ground and still seemed to be in a daze.

'What's wrong with him, Thomas? He won't talk to me. It's as if he doesn't know who I am.'

The cat turned his attention to James.

'It's worse than I thought, Emma. The magic he holds is an old magic. When the conjure was made long ago, the part made up of the dark arts was mixed with the good to make it work. They can reach him through that oldest of magic. We have to go very quickly now. I will do what I can. Let's hope it will be enough.'

Thomas sat in front of James and closed his eyes. Cranlow flew down and hung in the air just above the boy's head. The patch of white fur on the cat's shoulder began to glow. James looked into a beam of dazzling, white light. He cried out and tried to shield his eyes. The light streamed into James's body, filling him from the top of his head to the tip of his toes. Emma knelt beside him, trying to hold him as he slumped backwards and the light went out.

'That's it,' Thomas said eventually. 'He may be safe for a while, but we must hurry. Get him up on his feet, Emma, and watch him. If he strays from the path, they will have him. We must get out of this wood before dark.'

James stumbled as he walked. Emma tried to help him, but he pushed her away. Every few steps he hesitated, peering into the distance as if searching for something. All around them, the trees stretched away into an endless murk, gloomy and menacing. James uttered something under his breath and began to smile. Emma shuddered.

'Please let me help you, Jamie,' she said and held out her hands to him. 'See if we can't scare that old black dragon thing away.'

Thomas stopped in front of them so suddenly they almost fell over him.

'Don't you ever—not ever—say those words again! You must think before you speak, Emma.'

James stared at them both before sneering at Emma. The look on his face was cold-hearted and grim as he staggered away from them.

Something moved amongst the trees. They caught a fleeting glimpse of stick-like limbs and long shreds of filthy cloth, which flapped like a scarecrow's rags. James stopped and looked towards it. The woman he saw was even more beautiful than the fairy weaver. A voice whispered to him in the hidden places of his mind. He searched in his pocket for the talisman and flung it into the trees. Emma stepped towards him, but he wouldn't look at her. He turned instead towards the voice that was calling him. The sound was harsh and aggressive, but he only heard the honeyed voice of the trickster. Then, knowing there was nothing they could do to stop him, they watched helplessly as he walked into the treacherous grasp of his enemy.

Emma dropped to her knees in disbelief.

'How could this happen? Why didn't his dragon help him?'

'Wisp will help him, but he cannot risk himself. He must grow and learn so that he will be ready when his time comes, but without the talisman, he cannot reach James, and they know this.' Thomas replied.

'So what do we do now?' Emma felt hopeless.

For once, Thomas had nothing to say. The returning owl finally got them to move. Sensing the worst, he'd gone to find the wizard, which had seemed like good news until they saw Mr Witty.

'Well we've really had it now.' Thomas glared at Cranlow. 'Can't you get anything right? This is the wrong wizard!'

As Mr Witty bent over to speak to the cat, his hat fell off. It was red and had canary-yellow feathers tucked into the band on each side.

'See. Just look at that. What self-respecting wizard would be seen in that?'

Mr. Witty picked up his hat, quickly squashing it back onto his shiny, bald head as he said:

'Now. Now. We'll have less of that. Not you, Emma. Him.'

Even though she was so upset, Emma couldn't help but smile.

'What's going to happen to James? Oh, Mr Witty, please say you can help him.'

The wizard patted her on the arm.

'Well, my dear, we are certainly going to do our best. We need to get back inside that House. I'm certain that's where they've taken him. Cranlow will lead the way. We won't find him out here—that's for sure.—'

The owl finally stopped in front of a pile of fallen rocks. A cliff towered in front of them.

'Nice one,' muttered Thomas. 'Can't you do better than that?'

'Look again, cat,' Cranlow replied. 'What was that you were saying about how special you are?'

'Stop it, you two. Don't you think we've got enough trouble?' Emma stamped her foot in exasperation.

Mr Witty led them forwards and tapped a large stone with his staff. Nothing happened. He glared at the cat, who was shaking his head. The ground shuddered beneath their feet, and a large hole opened up. An iron ladder, covered in rust, led downwards into the darkness. They could hear the sound of rushing water.

'Right. Off you go, Cranlow. Check it out.' Mr Witty ordered.

'Who, me? Owls are not designed to fly into holes in the ground. We fly upwards, in case you hadn't noticed. If I go down there, I could run out of air pressure and—'

'Then you'd get wet,' Thomas interrupted.

'Well, you go then. Show everyone just how good you think you are.'

'We'll all go,' said Emma. 'So come on.'

The ladder ended at the entrance to a tunnel. The ground was wet beneath their feet as the river flowed past them flooding ever faster into a distant cavern. They were in total darkness. Not even Cranlow could lead them through that.

'But I can,' said Thomas. 'See. I told you I had special powers.'

Mr Witty cleared his throat. 'Not so fast, cat. You might be able to see in the dark, but we can't, so just hang on a minute.'

The wizard rummaged about in his cloak and produced a small, glass ball. Light streamed from it as he held it out in front of him.

'There. That should do it. Off you go then, Thomas.'

The tunnel led them ever further underground, following the river as it flowed into the depths. They hurried on, afraid to speak in case something might hear them. Every so often, they thought they heard whispering as unseen things scuttled about them in the darkness. Emma was becoming very frightened. In her mind, she could hear James calling out to her. She felt something touch her, making her jump. James was angry with her, blaming her. The voice was joined by another and another. Voices from the past telling her that she was no good.

She fell against the tunnel wall, quaking with fright as Mr Witty came towards her. She could hardly breathe.

'It's all right. Emma, it's me.'

He held out his hand to help her, but she dropped to the ground. Thomas sat beside her, purring loudly. She picked him up and burst into tears.

'It's them, Emma,' Mr Witty's face was filled with concern. 'They're trying to trick you like they have James. You have to trust me child, before it's too late.'

'He's right, you know,' said a very squeaky voice. 'Yes. We know, don't we?'

Robbit and Pest peeped out from behind the wizard's feet.

'You know what exactly? Something useful, I hope,' said Thomas.

'Oh, yes. I know and he knows, don't we?' They both nodded.

'Well, do tell,' said the cat. 'Or is this some kind of riddle?'

The mice looked at each other.

'A riddle?' they said. 'No, not that. But, what we know is '—they paused before whispering—'where he is. We know. We do.'

'What?' Emma managed to stand up.

'Oh yes.'

They were nodding again.

'Is he all right?'

The mice shook their heads as Emma feared the worst.

'We found it. We took it. He has it. He does.'

'Found what?' asked Mr Witty.

'It,' they said. 'In the woods. A little blue thing that wriggles. In his pocket. We put it. We did.'

Thomas groaned. Emma suddenly realised what they were trying to say.

'The talisman. They found the talisman.'

Mr Witty gave a large sigh of relief. 'Then we have some small hope. Quickly now. Show us where he is.'

James lay on the cold, damp floor of a cellar, concealed in the hidden depths beneath the House of Secrets. His dreams were more like nightmares. He could see Daisy reaching out to him and hear his mother weeping. Dark shapes moved around them. His breathing was shallow and laboured. The watcher poked him with its claw-like hand. James whimpered in his troubled sleep. The watcher poked him again, harder this time. James struggled to sit up. He opened his eyes but could see only the dreams. The watcher sniggered and pushed him back down, onto the cold, hard stones. A slight sound caught its attention, but it could see nothing and turned back to the boy. The creature was hungry. It reached towards James once more, then shrieked as pain shot through its arm. A blue haze was beginning to form around the boy. The watcher reached out to touch James again, but thought better of it and shrank back into the shadows, as the door flew open with a crash, and Mr Witty strode in. Cranlow, who was standing on top of the Great Book of Spells, dropped the heavy tome onto the watcher's head, just as it tried to sneak past them. The blue haze spread, filling the room, as the wizard lifted James into his arms.

'Hold on to me,' he shouted. 'Hold on tight!'

They could hear the sound of doors slamming shut all around them. Then the floor fell completely away. Emma heard herself screaming.

Emma was still screaming as they dropped into the circle of stones.

Mr Witty laid James very gently across the central altar stone. Although it was almost dawn, there was no light in the sky. Thunder rolled in the distance. The wizard took a small drum out of his bag. As he beat it, he began to chant, calling on the ancient guardians of the earth. Thomas, in the guise of the leopard, curled himself around James's unmoving body. The drum sounded like a heartbeat. He placed it on the ground and stood at James's head. Then, with his arms outstretched, he called out the boy's name, repeating it with every throb of the drum. Emma tried to join in, but he motioned her to stay back.

He called to all the spirits of the air, the earth, and the sea. Emma couldn't understand his words. They were rare and mysterious. The language of magic. As he chanted, the words ran together like a song, the sound rising and falling as his feet tapped in time and he circled the stone.

'Bring me the Book, Cranlow.'

The Great Book opened in front of the wizard. He touched it with his staff. Lightning sizzled across the ground as words lifted from the pages and hung in the air in front of him. Spells and incantations from a time lost to memory, buzzing with power. James began to breathe more easily. Thomas sat up, the white patch on his shoulder blazing with light. Images of the dancers filled James's mind. They were dancing to the oldest tune of all, but even as he watched, they faltered, missing the steps. As the images faded, he saw the Weaver. She took his hand and sang to him, leading him through a field of flowers. He felt himself floating, through the warmth of a summer breeze. As she sang, the turmoil lifted from his mind and the talisman throbbed with life, as the mind of the dragon found his. Someone was calling him. Someone he knew. It was the voice of his father.

James sat up. Thunder crashed all around them. Mr Witty was backing away from something they couldn't see. He was still chanting, but his power was fading fast. All the pages of the Great Book were blank. As the last of the spells drifted away, his staff shrivelled in his hands and dropped to the ground, where it lay withered and twisted before crumbling into powder and blowing away on the breeze. Fire flared through the stones towards him, revealing a blood-curdling demon, beating him back with its leathery wings. The wizard stumbled, falling to his knees, before summoning the last of his strength to bind the creature to him. It fought him, but he held it fast, dragging it with him as he struggled towards the edge of the circle, and beyond.

'Where is he?' asked Emma, when she realised he was no longer with them.

'He's gone,' said Thomas.

Emma didn't understand.

'Gone where?' she asked, still very confused.

James's voice was very weak and low as he said, 'He's dead, Emma. He's given his life to protect us. He's bought us some time.'

Emma knelt down beside him. She was too upset to speak. Thomas came and sat next to them.

The faint sound of bells drew their attention. The dancers were back, but this time they were outside the circle. The percussive sound of the sticks and the drum disrupted the air, creating a wave of energy. James could see it vibrating through the stones, connecting them with the magic of the earth. Through the eyes of the dragon, James watched as the stones began to move.

THE FORD OF MARA

They stood huddled together. A blustery wind was rising, driven by the movement of the stones. At first it didn't touch them as it gusted around the circle, becoming ever stronger and fiercer. Then it hit them full force, lifting them up, taking them higher and higher, twisting and tumbling through its buffeting roar. Emma was beginning to feel ill. Slowly, the wind eased until finally letting them drop. They'd landed on a hill overlooking a treeless valley. It was cold and late in the afternoon.

'Thank goodness for that.' Emma was rubbing her knees. 'Where are we?'

James shrugged. Thomas sat staring into the distance, and as usual, the owl was nowhere to be seen. A dark shape appeared on the horizon. As it approached, they could see it was a large, black bird.

'It's the raven,' said Thomas.

The bird landed on a nearby rock. It looked dangerous. The black feathers of its head and neck forming a ruff, making it seem even bigger. The sturdy, arched bill, specially designed to tear at dead meat, looked menacing. Thomas was keeping his distance.

'Welcome,' it croaked, 'I think you already know my name.'

It peered directly at James.

'Kark,' said James. 'It's Kark.'

'It is indeed. I will help to keep you on your path and act as your messenger. The owl will guide you where I cannot, but first, you should seek shelter in the house of Lehan. You must wait for the morning before attempting to cross the Ford of Mara and even then it will be extremely hazardous.'

He led them down the rocky hillside until they found a path leading to a stand of shrubby trees, within which stood a large, stone cottage. Welcoming light filled the single window on one side. The front door was painted the green of the forest, and a round, shiny brass knob hung from the bell pull. Cranlow flew towards them, like a great white moth in the darkening sky. As James reached up to ring the bell, the door opened, and a tall, fair-haired man stood in the doorway.

'Lehan Crow,' he said. 'At your service. I've been expecting you.'

A warm fire crackled in the hearth, and the table was laid ready.

'I hope you're hungry,' said the man. 'I know I am.'

Later, as they sat dozing, full and sleepy, the man motioned them to follow him. He led them up a flight of stairs into a small, circular room, which had windows all around it.

'Look out,' he said to James. 'And tell me what you see.'

'There's nothing to see,' said Emma, who had her nose pressed up against the glass.

James was scratching his head.

'Look again,' said Lehan Crow.

'Lights,' said James. 'But they're moving.'

'Fireflies,' said the man. 'Look beyond them.'

James peered further into the darkness, straining his eyes. Then he gasped.

'Colours,' he said. 'Like on a map, only more. And it sparkles like it was sprinkled with precious stones.'

'Stardust,' said Lehan. 'Find the colour of your way and remember it. It's the way of the dragon. The colour he'll know.'

'Blue,' said James. 'It's blue like the sky.'

Lehan Crow smiled and nodded.

'It's better that both you and Cranlow can see your way. But now you must rest, for tomorrow your journey begins.'

The following morning was cold. Frost crunched beneath their feet. A dense fog filled the valley, muffling all sound.

'How will we find the way now?' Emma was worried. 'Cranlow can't fly in this.'

Lehan Crow touched James on the shoulder.

'Come,' he said. 'Let's see what you can find.'

James followed him onto the hillside behind the cottage, not feeling at all confident, but as he searched, he detected the glow. A faint ribbon of flickering, blue light marked their path across the frosty ground.

Lehan nodded. 'Good. But now you must learn what awaits you at the Ford and how to deal with her. She is known as the Maiden of Mara, but a maid she most certainly is not. She will try her hardest to stop you from crossing and make you her prisoners. Once, a very long time ago, she was a beautiful young woman, but she was greedy and jealous of others, wanting to steal their possessions. She rejected all those who sought to befriend her, causing them misfortune and harm, some even to their deaths. As time passed and her cruel deeds multiplied, the dark forces that threaten us now, drew her into their midst. Each awful deed bound her ever more tightly, as her beauty faded and she became the awful monstrosity you're about to encounter.'

'What if we can't avoid her and she gets us?' asked James, dreading the answer.

'No one has ever escaped from her lair under the shaded hill,' replied Lehan. 'So you have to beat her, and there is a way. It is the only way.'

Thomas didn't like water very much, and the prospect of swimming appealed to him even less. He knew of the Maiden and how nasty she was, and kept very quiet indeed.

'She had a mirror,' continued Lehan, 'with which, in her vanity, she spent hour after hour admiring herself. No matter how ugly she became, the mirror still showed her the likeness of her youth. One day, she dropped it. Her frantic searching revealed nothing, until a brilliant flash of sunlight caught her eye as it toppled over the nearby waterfall. In the days before she became the watcher at the ford, people used to come and bathe in the pool beneath the falls, as it was believed the water could heal them if they were ill. In absolute desperation, she dived into the pool to search for it. The water burned her, making her scream and writhe until at last, she found it and ran back to the Ford, turning the water red with her blood. She raised the mirror to her face, then let out a sickening shriek as she saw the horror it revealed.

She looked again and fell to her knees, moaning and wailing, as she recognised the revolting image as herself. In fury, she threw the mirror as far away as she could, where it hit a rock and shattered as it sank into the depths. As time passed, she regretted her action, craving just one more look, but no matter how hard she searched, she could never find it.'

'The mirror was made of crystal and dewdrops, held together by elven spells. The healing waters had changed it to reveal the truth when before, it had deceived her just as she had deceived so many herself. You must find it and let her look into it. But do not let her hold it. Her dreadful image may stop her and give you the chance to get through. That is all I know. After that, you must take assistance where it is found. Now go. I can help you no more.'

'Can't you do something?' James asked Thomas, who was lagging behind.

'Wrong kind of magic. This is more your simple earth type. Besides, she got what she deserved, so who am I to interfere?'

'Not a whole lot of help then,' said Emma.

'No,' said James as he called out to Thomas. 'Catch up. We're all supposed to be in this together, remember?'

The cat ignored them but thought better of it as they approached the Ford.

'Slow down,' he insisted. 'Let's see what's going on. We need to get closer. She'll be there somewhere, waiting to grab us if she gets the chance.'

Even at the water's edge, there was no sign of her.

'We have to cross. We have to,' James muttered as he led them into the deepening water.

They had almost reached halfway when a sudden movement stopped them in their tracks. Brown, muddy water seethed around their legs as the Maiden pushed herself up to tower over them.

Her hair was matted and covered in green slime, which dripped down her face and into her fiercely staring eyes. Strips of rotting cloth clung to her shapeless body. Blood dripped from her wounds as she lunged towards them.

'Ah, my pretty creatures. So young. Soo tender. Sooo sweet.'

Her breath was foul, like the stench from the bottom of a festering bog, as she spoke through broken stumps of blackened teeth.

Thomas was changing his form again, this time into a massive swarm of furious, stinging bees, which covered her almost completely. She backed away, swatting at the painful stingers before immersing herself in the water hoping to drown them. Then back she came, reaching for Emma.

'Come now. Let me look at you.'

Her clutching, claw-like hands grabbed Emma, lifting her out of the water as she struck at James, narrowly missing his head. He knew she wouldn't miss again. Thomas was caught in the current as he fought his way back to them. Revulsion threatened to overwhelm James as pointed, razor-sharp talons slashed towards him. Emma was too scared even to scream. The Maiden shook her as if she were a rag doll as she lunged at James again. A sound cut through his fear as the voice of Kob filled his mind.

'The whistle,' he was saying. 'Use the whistle!'

James closed his eyes, pictured a mirror, and blew. Slivers of crystal and glass drifted towards him through the murky water as the mirror began to reform. He blew a little harder, waiting until it floated in front of him, then quickly snatched it to him from under the Maiden's nose. She screeched, dropping Emma, as she staggered backwards with shock.

'Run!' Emma shouted, trying to pull James with her. 'James, run!'

His legs refused to move. The Maiden slid towards him as he desperately tried to back away, but he was stuck fast. She held out her long, piercing talons as she begged him to give her the mirror.

'No!' he cried out in a terrified voice. 'You can never have it!'

She stopped, scared that he would throw it away, knowing that it would then be lost forever.

'I must!' she cried. 'Give it to me! It's mine!'

'No!' shouted James. 'But if you stay where you are, and don't come any closer, I might let you look into it.'

She stood, shaking her foul head. Finally, vanity overcame her and she leaned towards him. James lifted the mirror, holding onto it as tightly as he could. He could hardly bear to look at her as she peered eagerly into it. Her eyes bulged, and dirty, mud-filled tears slid down her face as the disgusting freak she had become stared back at her.

She dashed them away, making a ghastly gurgling noise, which sounded as if she were choking. James still couldn't move. The Maiden made a sudden, desperate rush towards him, snatching at the mirror. As she touched it, a tiny sliver of crystal detached itself, piercing her skin. She tried to pull it out, but it burrowed deep into her flesh. At last, James found he could move.

They reached the bank on the other side and kept on running until they thought they were at a safe distance, before daring to look back. The Maiden was frantically thrashing about in the filthy, seething water. It boiled and fizzed all around her as she slowly dissolved into it. Then, with one final piercing shriek, she sank out of sight into the inky, smoking depths.

JOURNEY TO THE FORTRESS OF THE MOON

Cranlow had been waiting for them together with Kark. The Raven took off and circled above them before coming back to land.

'The Dark Wood of Scretch lies in our path. It is not a large wood, but many have been lost in it, never to return. It is bewitched and full of illusions, which trick the mind of the unwary.'

'Well. Can't we go around it?' asked James.

'We could, but we would have to travel a very long way to avoid its influence, and you don't really have the time to do that, do you?'

James shook his head as he realised he was still holding the mirror and quickly shoved it into his rucksack, too unnerved to look into it. Water was running out of Thomas's coat, making a pool on the ground as he said grumpily, 'What about that dragon of yours? He can see the way through. That's what Lehan Crow said. Speak to him, James. It's about time he did something useful.'

'He can hear you, Thomas,' said James.

'Good. So let's go then. Come on! Oh, and let's not forget our intrepid navigator. Eh, Cranlow. What have you got to say for yourself?'

'Only that I will do my best,' hooted the Owl. 'As always.'

Thomas was just about to make another jeering remark when Kark took off again.

'We must leave, ' he said. 'Without delay. There are those who follow.'

'Is that a village over there?' asked Emma, pointing towards the edge of the trees.

'The village of Scretch,' Kark replied. 'I will go ahead of you. There is one there with whom I need to speak. You must wait here for my return.'

Thomas kept looking behind them.

'What is it?' asked Emma as she peered into the distance.

'We have to go now.' Thomas stared directly at James.

'We can't. Kark said to wait for him. Look. Here he is.'

'Our followers are just over that ridge behind us,' the Raven croaked. 'We shall have to make a detour to avoid them. They are swift travellers, so we must make haste. They are tracking us through the dark magic James holds. We will seek help before we go on.'

He led them into the village and down a narrow, cobbled lane to an old, tumbledown cottage with a roof thatched with straw-coloured reed. No windows looked onto the lane, and the only door was at the back. They hurried in to be greeted by a creature that looked a bit like Kob.

'Sit here,' he said to James as he pulled out a chair.

'I am Klin, Kob is my kin. Bad things come. We must make you a charm to deceive them.'

He looked towards the owl, who had landed on the table in front of them and was staring straight into James's face.

'Cranlow will guide you. We need another to assist us, and only he can find him.'

'How will he do that?' asked James.

'Ah,' said Klin mysteriously. 'This owl can see what others can't and go where others may not follow.'

Klin lit a mixture of herbs in a shallow bowl, and as James breathed in the sweet-smelling smoke, he began to feel drowsy. His body felt weightless as he watched the owl who was gliding before him. He felt as if he were floating through the air with him. A drum sounded somewhere in the distance together with the lighter tone of wind chimes. Cranlow flew onwards towards the sounds as the beat of the drum increased.

The figure of a man sat cross-legged on the ground in front of them. Orange powder covered his face and hands. The outline of each of his eyes was blackened with charcoal. His thick, red hair was plaited like dreadlocks and hung down to his waist. The image of a wolf was tattooed on his chest and across his back, an eagle. His only clothing was a pair of short, brown trousers made of animal hide. Coloured beads, hung on a string around his neck, together with the teeth of a bear and the skull of a shrew.

As they approached, he lifted his head, turning towards James. Where his eyes should have been were empty, chalk-white sockets, the eyes of a blind ghost. Then James knew they were in the place of the spirits.

The shaman crouched in front of a small fire, from which he scooped up crumbly, grey ashes, smearing them over his body. The drum James had heard lay next to him. Winged horses were painted onto its sides. He placed a thin, cotton mat on the ground where James was to sit, before blowing the ash into his face and onto his hair.

Cranlow perched above the wind chimes in a nearby tree which was hung with paper lanterns. The shaman began to chant, beating the painted drum. James fell into a trance as the pounding of the drum called to the spirit helpers. Figures formed in the spiralling smoke of the fire, making a circle around them. James's gaze was fixed on the blind shaman as he picked up a bone rattle and knelt in front of him. As he shook it, he touched James's head, eyes, and lips with the feather of a wren. The Shaman's eyes held James spellbound in their sightless gaze.

Then someone was shaking him. It was Klin. Thomas, who had been sitting on his lap, jumped down to the floor. Cranlow was perched on the back of a chair, his huge, gold-flecked eyes blinking slowly as he waited for James to recover.

'Well done,' said Klin. 'I think that was quite a journey. I see you have the charm. It will help, but don't take it for granted. It will not shield you from more determined of seekers.'

'There's something around your neck,' said Emma, pointing.

James put his hand up and touched a small, cloth bag.

'Never take it off,' warned Klin. 'It is your protection, so you must treat it with care.'

'What's in it?' asked Emma.

'Spells,' replied Klin. 'Rare herbs and symbols of magic. Ah. Here is Kark. He has been watching so that you may leave safely.'

'It is time,' croaked the raven. 'The way is clear for now.'

Thomas looked towards Cranlow, who seemed to have fallen asleep yet again.

'Probably best to just leave him here. Looks like he's too tired to be bothered.'

The owl yawned loudly.

'Old age,' said Thomas. 'It does that, you know.'

Cranlow took off.

'I'll go on ahead. No need to hang about waiting for you. And,' he added, swooping low over Thomas's head, 'I think I can safely say that you, are most definitely the oldest of us all. Goodbye.'

James was grinning as he thanked Klin and they made their way out into the lane.

'So what happened?' asked Emma. 'You looked as if you were asleep, but your eyes were wide open.'

Thomas answered for him, 'Well. Hard as it may be to believe, that owl has the magic of the moon, which lets him travel in the realm of the supernatural as, of course, can I. He, however, can take your spirit with him. That's where James has been, to meet with Mercriel, a shaman of great power. Only he could tap into the dark magic locked inside James's mind.'

'Let's hope it works then.' James shuddered as he remembered the shaman's sightless eye sockets.

As they approached the wood, Cranlow flew towards them.

'There are searchers near,' he said. 'They must not see you. Come, we must hide.'

He led them to a low, moss-covered wall, behind which they crouched hoping their pursuers would not find them.

The sticklike horror that had trapped James before was in the lead, followed by the foulest of creatures. Vraga were amongst them, tasting the air for the scent of the warm blood they craved.

Emma, shaking with fright, was huddled close to the base of the wall, not daring to look. As the others watched, the trees seemed to shift, changing the route of the path, leading the horrible horde away. The noise of their passing faded, and Kark called them out of their hiding place.

The wood appeared harmless enough. Sunlight filtered through the trees, and the path was wide and clear. As they walked further into the wood, they began to notice the silence. No birds sang; not even the lightest breeze rustled in the leaves. A veil of mist began to rise, blurring their way as it became darker and noticeably colder. They stopped. Something skittered about on the path ahead of them.

'Why have we stopped?' asked Emma.

'Because I can't see the trail.'

James's voice was almost a whisper as fingers of fear clutched at his throat. Cranlow hovered in front of them as Kark joined him.

'Neither can we,' said the Raven. 'And we can't fly above the treetops to look for it.'

The cat's eyes flashed before he disappeared from sight. James's hand closed over the talisman as he called to the dragon for help. It was hot, but he held onto it tightly. There was no sign of Thomas as they searched for the path. Wisp rumbled in his mind, but try as they might, there was nothing to see. The mist thickened, spreading through the trees all around them. Behind them came the sounds of fighting. James and the dragon peered further into the trees. Pinpoints of light flickered in the mist as dark, misshapen figures rushed towards them.

'It's there. Look. It's there,' called James, just as Thomas hurled himself at them.

'Hurry! There are too may. I can't stop them!'

They blundered into the trees at the very last minute as their pursuers, shouting and clattering, sped past without seeing them.

'They are bewitched,' said Kark. 'And thankfully, the charm has kept you hidden from them. All they will see now are phantoms. But we must be very careful, or we could become trapped as well.'

They trudged on through the wood for mile after endless mile. They were tired, and Emma's feet were hurting. In the pitch black only James could see the faint line of the path at first, until Cranlow picked up the silver thread of the earth magic, which made his feathers glow just enough for them to follow. No one spoke. The silence was as thick as treacle.

Gradually, the trees began to thin out, and a stiff breeze was blowing as they emerged into daylight. The wind was cold, and frost glittered on the heathery turf of the ground in front of them.

Emma shivered as they walked on towards a large outcrop of rock.

'How much further?' She wanted to stop. 'Just where is this fortress thing anyway?'

Thomas watched as Kark flew towards them.

'Ask him,' he said.

The raven drifted in front of them, his feathers stirred up by the wind.

'It's not where it was,' he croaked. 'The entrance used to be at the foot of those hills over there, but there's no sign of it now.'

'There has to be something,' said Thomas. 'Some small trace of it we can follow.'

'There's nothing here,' said James as they approached the hills. 'Just nothing.'

Thomas sat staring at a large boulder, which jutted out of the rock face.

'I'm not so sure,' he said. 'I think you need to ask that dragon.'

James took the talisman out of his pocket. As he approached the boulder, it began to hum, becoming the blue of the path they were following.

'I knew it,' said Thomas. 'Well, go on. Ask him.'

As James touched the stone, he saw where they had to go. The image the dragon showed him was very clear.

'Well?' said Thomas. 'Give us a clue then. Where is it?'

James hung his head. 'It's impossible,' he said very quietly. 'It's too far away. We're never going to be able to get there.'

'Well, tell us anyway,' said Emma, her foot tapping with impatience.

'We have to cross the sea,' he said, utterly despondently. 'It's on the other side of the world.'

An odd sound caused them to turn and look up. High in the sky, a creature was speeding towards them. It bugled again. Thomas was the first to realise what it was.

'It's that so-called dragon. First he breathes fire, and now he can fly. Whatever next, I wonder? Look out! He's coming in to land, and who's that on his back?'

'It's the Master,' said James, relieved to know that help had finally arrived.

Wisp had never made a proper landing before and was approaching too fast. His feet paddled the air like a goose on take-off, and his wings back-pedalled frantically as he tried to slow himself down. They hurried out of his way as he thundered to a halt, just in time to avoid crashing into the rocks. The Master slid off the dragon's back. He was chuckling to himself.

'Well done,' he said. 'Just a little more practice, I think.'

Wisp turned towards them. He was truly enormous. Smoke curled from his nostrils, and the scales on his back gleamed with the same intense blue as the talisman.

'Did you make that sound?' asked Emma.

James nodded. 'Oh yes,' he replied, feeling the dragon's amusement.

'Do tell us why you're here,' said Thomas, keeping a safe distance.

'He's your transport,' said the Master, stroking the dragon's neck.

Thomas was was lost for words as James shook his head in disbelief.

'How does he know where to take us?' asked Emma.

'He doesn't. The place you seek is not in this world. But first you must find your way to the Fortress of the Moon. James and the dragon can see over water. Thomas will search also, in ways only he knows, and Cranlow will follow the signs of the earth. I will remain to delay those who are trying to stop you. Now go.'

They climbed onto Wisp's wide back and held on tightly, as the dragon's powerful wings lifted them high above the clouds, flying into the unknown. They flew through the rest of the day and across the starlit sky of the night, tracing the curve of the earth as the dragon followed the path, which, at this height, only he could see. Emma had fallen asleep, and James dozed quietly as they crossed the face of the moon. It was then that the dragon began his descent, making great circles as he dived towards the surface of the ocean.

Emma woke with a start. It was like coming down from the top of the big wheel at the fair, only faster. She was beginning to feel sick as her tummy threatened to jump out of her throat.

They were heading towards a small island, an outcrop of rock in the sea. James hung tightly onto Wisp's neck. He could just make out the faint blue of their pathway as they found a place to land. Thomas was the first to jump off the dragon's back.

'Well. Isn't this just what we wanted? To be marooned on an island in the middle of some nameless ocean.'

Wisp blew smoke at him, making him cough.

'Look,' said James pointing. 'Over there. Looks like steps cut into the face of the cliff.'

The steps were steep and uneven. Cranlow flew up the stairway before returning to tell them to follow.

'Not that again,' muttered Thomas. 'Remember the last time you said that? I think we do.'

'Of course you could always stay here,' hooted the owl. 'Then you really would be marooned.'

They followed, keeping close together. Kark hovered above them. The steps led into a narrow passageway, which opened out into a paved courtyard. The Fortress of the Moon towered in front of them, bleak and forbidding. As Wisp forced himself through, rocks fell behind him, blocking their way back.

'Oh, well done,' sneered Thomas before turning to James. 'It looks about the same as always, I think.'

'You've been here before?'

'A very long time ago,' the cat replied.

'So how do we get in then?'

'We have to be invited,' said Thomas. 'They know we are here.'

James turned to Wisp, who bent his huge head to be patted. Lights were approaching, followed by others as a group of young women walked towards them. They stopped, waiting.

'We must go with them,' said Thomas.

The women seemed to float above the ground, their robes shimmering with a pale, rosy glow as they lead them towards an unwelcoming, steel-barred door, which creaked slowly open to allow them to enter. They were in a long hall with what looked like at least a hundred doors on either side of it. The young women turned to them in greeting, as the tallest and fairest of them said, 'We welcome you, but from here you must find your own way through. The Fortress of the Moon holds many mysteries and secret places. There are those amongst us who would not be pleased you are here, and others who would seek to deceive you. This is where the magic of the moon is strongest, but beware. You must trust your instincts and each other. Stay together no matter what, as your way is beset with trickery. Remember this: the moon is both the giver and the taker of life. Now we must leave you. Go well.'

They stared, with mounting anxiety, at the doors as the women left.

'Got any ideas?' asked James.

Thomas just sat staring at Cranlow who was perched on a chandelier.

'What about the talisman?' asked Emma.

James shook his head, knowing for some reason he couldn't explain, that it wouldn't help, even though the dragon was there with them.

'What about you?' called James as Cranlow began to glide around the hall. Multicoloured bubbles flowed from his feathers as he flew.

The owl inspected three of the doors before landing in front of the middle one.

'There would appear to be something here,' he hooted.

'And I'll bet my whiskers it won't be what we want,' Thomas muttered as he strutted over to the owl.

'S'pose we'd better try it then.'

James opened the door, which led into another large room with yet more doors. They tried again, but the result was the same.

'We're trapped,' said Emma. 'We'll never get out of here at this rate. All the rooms are the same.'

James felt an ever increasing sense of dread as they entered room number 6. However, this time, the choice was made for them as there was only one large door. It led through an iron grille into a squat, square tower. As the door slammed behind them, they heard the lock click loudly into place. In the middle of the floor was a gaping hole from which a threadbare rope descended into the gloom. Thomas stared over the edge before backing quickly away.

'I thought you said you'd been here before,' said James. 'So why don't you know where we have to go?'

'It was different then. There used to be Guardians here, but they have gone along with the creatures of light that lived here too. Even here the power is waning, letting in the shadows of the dark.'

'We'll have to go down,' said James. 'Shall I carry you? This doesn't look very safe.'

'No need,' said Thomas. 'But I will go first.'

'And I will follow,' hooted Cranlow. 'Then Emma, James, and the dragon—if he can get through.'

James watched as Thomas's smoke-like form drifted downwards. Cranlow waited, his wings glowing below them as they made their way down. Instead of doors, passageways led everywhere. It was like being in the middle of a maze.

'What's that?' whispered Emma as she craned her head to listen. 'Sounds like a baby crying.'

'Not here,' said Thomas. 'Not possible.'

'Yes, there is. Listen. It's down there.' Emma was really anxious now.

Before they could stop her, she'd hurried away from them.

'Come back!' shouted James, but she'd gone.

A child turned to face her as she rounded a corner. A pretty, fair-haired little girl.

'Was that you I heard?' asked Emma as the child reached for her hand. The child nodded.

'Please,' she said. 'Come and play with me. I'm so lonely here. Let me show you where I live.'

Emma pulled back as the child drew her onwards.

'It's near the way out,' the child tempted.

'No. I must wait for my friends.'

'But they are here,' said the child, pulling her forward. Please let me take you.'

A black shape appeared, followed by James. The child stopped, dropping Emma's hand.

'It's only a little girl,' said James, thinking of how like Daisy she looked.

'I think not.' Thomas's dark shape flowed around the child, who cowered away.

'Look at her in your mirror, James. Then you'll see what she really is.'

James found the mirror buried at the bottom of his pack and held it up in front of the child. What it revealed made him jump back in absolute astonishment.

'It can't be!' he cried, finding it hard to believe what the mirror was showing him.

'Oh, but it can,' said Thomas. 'Meet Rameel, and yes, he really is an angel but a very bad one, are you not? Always ready to cause trouble with his lies and deceits.'

Emma gasped as the angel's true shape was revealed, hostile and menacing.

'Your tricks don't fool me,' said Thomas. 'Now go before I let those who seek you know where you hide. Your deeds have not gone unnoticed.'

The angel laughed. The sound was empty and cold. They left him there, the sound echoing behind them as they followed Cranlow back to where they'd started.

Every corridor they tried was a dead end, and they were becoming very scared. Even Cranlow couldn't find their way.

'It's hopeless.' Emma was in tears.

A huge, black spider suddenly dropped from the ceiling in front of them, making her shriek.

'Schlema,' said Thomas. 'We must hope she will help.'

The spider swung lower on her silken line as the cat spoke to her, in a very strange language indeed.

'Look,' cried Emma, pointing. 'There are thousands of them.'

There were spiders everywhere. Wisp tried his best not to squash any.

'They will spin, and we must follow the threads. Cranlow can see the moon magic in them, but first, you must thank her, James. Schlema is the queen of them all and weaver of the web of the world. I believe you've met her once before.'

James remembered, but he wasn't sure how to speak to a spider so was as polite as he knew how. Emma thanked her too before they followed the speeding owl. Doors slammed as they passed certain places, and sometimes they glimpsed figures scurrying out of their way. Bats squeaked above their heads as a faint, glimmer of light showed in the distance.

As they emerged from the Fortress, James noticed that Kark wasn't with them.

'He's gone back,' said Thomas. 'Been called by Kallen Lupus to report and to let your family know how things are with you.'

The thought of his family made James sad.

'I wish I was there,' he said quietly. 'I wish I could talk to my dad.'

'Let's hope you will,' said Thomas. 'And before too long, if all goes well.'

The moon was full and bright; making everything look as if it were coated in silver. The talisman wriggled as James touched it. He closed his eyes, remembering what Michael, the Keeper of the Stones, had told him.

'Look for the place where light shimmers through air. Feel the tingle, like pins and needles in your fingers and a prickling on your face. The place where time shifts through space.'

He held out his hands.

'It's here,' he said as they gathered around him. 'Keep close together and follow me.'

THE CAVE OF THE WINDS

The ancient dragon lay silent, and as still as stone in his secret den, deep in the dreamless slumber of enchantment, waiting for the call that would change everything.

The underground cavern in which he slept was illuminated by the faint glow of phosphorous, which coated the walls. The only sound, the steady lapping of water from ripples in a nearby pool.

On a moss-covered stone, not far from the dragon's head, stood a large drum, the sides of which were studded with priceless jewels and stars made of solid gold. The Great Drum of Glav, crafted by dwarves in a time long forgotten. Silent now but ready, marking time before the dreaded call.

The Old One also slept, suspended in a bubble of flawless crystal, floating freely in that timeless, hidden place.

Touched by a strange disquiet, the dragon stirred. The tip of his tail moved disturbing the edge of a ripple in the pool. Slowly, the water began to brighten as if lit from below. As the light increased, the water became infused with colour; ruby, emerald, blue and gold spreading across the surface of the swelling ripples. The colours lifted, curling over the dragon's back, filling its dull, brown scales with ever-deepening shades until they glistened, as if sprinkled with the precious dust of stars. As the colours intensified, so the jewels on the great drum began to glitter and shine.

The dragon moved again and drew in a long, deep breath as the surface of the drum started to vibrate, his charmed sleep of ages, drawing to a close.

A sound like the rumbling of thunder, distant at first then growing ever louder, shook the air around them as the Great Drum of Glav began to sound.

Zramanth, the Magnificent, ancient guardian of the Old One and his mysteries, keeper of secrets and the mightiest of his kind, was awake.

On the other side of the pool stood a boy, who was staring at him with his mouth open. As he watched, others appeared. Then he saw Wisp and knew that the final test was upon them all.

Emma was dumbstruck with amazement and wonder. She had never thought she'd ever see a creature so big. Thomas sat very still and quiet in the background. James looked through Wisp's eyes as he came face-to-face with his future, and knew that he was scared too.

Zramanth stood up and leaned towards them. He looked as if he could finish them off in a second. James felt Wisp's fear as he lifted his head to touch the ancient dragon's forehead. A shudder passed through the ground, causing the Old One's crystal bubble to tip and drop to the floor.

As it landed, James knew the magic that held it could only be broken by a certain sound. He also knew the only way to make that sound was to use the golden flute, and he was filled with dread. He hesitated, trying not to remember the last time he'd attempted to use it, before putting it to his lips and closing his eyes tightly. Kob had taught him well. He filled his mind with the vision of the Old One as the magical notes began to appear. The sound was rich and full, like the deep, base chords played on an old-fashioned organ. The notes spread, winding themselves around the crystal before melting into it. The Old One sighed as he broke out of his enchanted sleep and the crystal cracked open like an egg. An old man stood before them, his beard so long it touched the floor. He was small, not much taller than James. The most powerful wizard of them all.

'And so the time has come at last.' His voice was deep and low.

As he spoke, his crumpled, black cloak smoothed itself out, and glowing, magical designs spun themselves into its fabric. He stepped towards James, putting his hands on his shoulders.

'First we must see if your dragon is ready. Come,' he called to Wisp. 'Let me look at you.'

Wisp almost knelt in front of him as the Old One inspected him closely.

'Is he?' he asked, turning his attention to Zramanth.

'Yes. He knows your name. It is as I thought, so we must begin.'

The wizard drew a slim, hazel wand from inside his cloak and began to chant, motioning the two dragons to face each other.

Wisp seemed to be getting bigger as Zramanth diminished, his colours fading as they passed to Wisp. The wizard touched the dragon with his wand, and as he did so, it breathed a fire of cold, blue flame out of which letters formed into the name that would replace Wisp's forever. The flaming letters hung in the air above Wisp's head before quickly burning themselves into his skin.

'So be it,' said the Old One. 'It is done.'

He looked very sad.

'Now you must go and leave me to say goodbye to my most faithful of companions. I will join you for the final test.'

'What will happen to him?' asked James.

'He will rest, with all those who came before him, until the end of our time, and his sleep will be a peaceful one. Do not fear for him. He has just come to the end of his journey, as do we all.'

They made their way back to the gate with heavy hearts as a tempest rose up behind them, violent and wild, pounding the Cave of the Winds with such force that everything in it was turned into dust, and it ceased to exist.

THE CIRCLE OF POWER

Michael greeted them as they entered the Place of Dreams. Within the Circle of Power, the stones stood cold and still. Mr Fairweather and the dancers weaved through them, the energy of the dance waking the wild magic of the Guardians, the rhythmic force of the drum guiding their steps.

The dragon they still knew as Wisp stood in the centre, Kallen Lupus and the Old One on either side of him, reaching out to touch his half-furled wings. He was ready as he stood, proud and magnificent, his scales reflecting all the colours of light.

A creature approached from the desolate land beyond the stones. Behind it, a fearsome horde spread out as far as the eye could see. They moved forward in silence. Thunder clapped above them as the sky grew ever darker. Lightning struck the ground in front of them, halting them, but not for long. The lightning flashed again, and James gasped as he recognised the loathsome creature that led them. The Black Dragon, the destroyer, the unspeakable beast revealed through the eyes of Wisp when they had first met.

The horde spread out, their approach made even more menacing by their silence. When they reached the outer edge of the Circle, they stopped and began to chant.

The Master and the Old One walked towards them. In his hand, the Old One carried a wand of ash, the wood of purity and cleansing. Cranlow hovered soundlessly behind him, bubbles of magic floating from his wings.

The fearsome war chant increased in volume as the terrifying horde clashed their weapons and stomped their feet, creating a wave of sound that exploded towards them. The dancers hit each stone with the striking sticks as Mr Fairweather beat out a changing rhythm on the drum, blending with the sound of the bells.

The Black Dragon bellowed in challenge. Emma hid behind Wisp, too scared to look. White smoke curled from his nostrils as he bent his head towards James. Their heads touched, and the awesome strength of the dragon coursed through him, connecting with the secrets in his mind.

The stones began to move, slowly at first but increasing in speed until they were a blur, creating a sound like the roar of a raging waterfall.

The Black Dragon bellowed again, rearing up as it urged its ruthless followers forward. A storm of fire sprang up around it as Michael drew his avenging sword.

Wisp opened his wings ready to attack, but Mr Fairweather held him back. James felt the dragon's overwhelming urge to fight and knew that he must stop him.

'No!' he cried. 'No! Wait! You must wait!'

Wisp bugled his defiance. Fire blazed in his stomach and up through his chest.

'No!' James shouted again. Fear giving extra volume to his voice. 'Stop! You must stop!'

The dragon slowly calmed, and the fire within him dimmed, but his tail swished back and forth in agitation as he tried to control himself. Mr Fairweather pulled Emma out of harm's way.

James felt the dragon's emotion. It was anger. An anger so strong it could make him do something reckless, an action they could all live to regret. At this moment, he was even more dangerous than the unspeakable force that threatened them.

It was then James heard the voice of the Weaver. She was singing a song so hauntingly beautiful he began to weep. He called to Wisp through his tears, holding out his arms to him. The dragon dropped his troubled head into James's hands as Seremela's gentle voice soothed him, and the song faded slowly away.

The sky became even darker, as if it were endless night and the moon had hidden its face from the world.

The stones were beginning to change. The spirit of the Guardians surged through them, as all the power of the earth rose up to touch the universe.

The horde drew ever closer, almost ready to break through. Michael advanced, his flaming sword ringing out as he attacked. For a split second, the Black Dragon fell back, but his foul, followers pushed him onwards, taunting and jeering. As they drove forward again, the cone of power began to dim.

The smoky shape of Thomas moved to stand behind Michael. He was calling out a name. He called it three times. The name was Chamael, the name of the spirit in the land of the dead. He called it again, louder this time. Chamael, archangel of healing and protector of the earth, appeared before him.

'Your time has come,' said Thomas. 'Now you may choose on which side you fight. Choose well.'

As the angel moved towards the Master, his shadowy form gradually turned into that of a tall, young man with light-blonde hair and startling green eyes. He wore a dark-brown habit, gathered in at the waist by a sturdy, knotted rope. In his hand he held a sword of burnished steel. His bare feet hardly touched the ground as he took his place beside Michael.

The shrieking horde were beating Michael back. Fire burst through the air as the Black Dragon tried to blast its way through, slowing the spinning stones, creating an entrance for its hideous army.

Now Wisp moved forward, meeting fire with fire. More of the horde were breaking through, trampling over their fallen as they gained ground. The cone of power dimmed even more as the stones slowed. Suddenly, from high within the cone, came horses. Great, white horses with dazzling, silver wings. Riding the lead horse was the figure of a man, wearing a lime-green robe and two gaudy, scarlet feathers in the band of his hat. Behind them came eagles, true creatures of magic, carrying with them the avenging spirits of the earth. Cold fire, cleansing and pure, radiated from amongst them, as riding shafts of lightning, they directed it into the deadly horde.

Gradually, the Black Dragon began to lose ground, and its gruesome army started to fall. It bellowed with rage as Michael's flaming sword bit into its putrid flesh. With each bite of the sword, Michael's strength increased; as with Chamael beside him, the angels beat the wicked creature back.

The Old One called out to James as he touched Wisp with his staff.

'Now!' he shouted. 'The time is now!'

Forgotten magic flowed through James as he and Wisp together caste the ancient spell. The dragon's true name entered James's mind. A name formidable and mighty: Azramoth Mazrael, a guardian and the chosen follower of Zramanth the Magnificent.

The chaos of magic split the air as James shouted the name at the top of his voice and the dragon launched himself into the fight.

The horde retreated as the attack strengthened. With each backwards step, the Black Dragon began to change, revealing its true, monstrous identity, the shape in which it became vulnerable to Michael's unforgiving blade and knew that this time, there would be no escape. As Michael raised his sword to strike its final, mortal blow, James shouted Wisp's true name once more, reaching out to touch the Master, joining the magic, connecting them all to the spinning cone of power.

A blinding flash of light, brighter than the sun, knocked them off their feet as forgotten magic drew the dragon, that once was Wisp, up into the dazzling cone. Through his eyes, James watched as all the damage done began to heal and the sky grew bright again. And Wisp was gone, changed forever, fulfilling his destiny within the Circle of Power together with all the others of his kind.

James felt him leave as with one last gentle rumble, he went on his way.

'I'll never forget you,' he whispered.

Emma reached out to hold James's hand, sensing the depth of his sadness as everyone gathered around them.

'Nor will he forget you,' said the Old One, as he put his arm around James's shoulders. 'And just maybe, one day, you might meet him again. Nothing is impossible, they say.'

Horses and eagles circled around them, slowly rising up into the sky, as the angels joined them. The wizards raised their staffs in farewell as the lead horse landed in front of James.

'It can't be,' whispered Emma. 'Can it?'

Mr Witty raised his hat, which now sported two different feathers: one violet, the other the colour of a tangerine.

Thomas yawned loudly.

Well, you've managed to get something right at last, but nothing's changed, I see.'

The horse pawed the ground in front of the cat. With each touch of its glittering hooves, the ground glinted with flickering sparks. Thomas shook his head as he moved back. Mr Witty just ignored him as usual.

'Good to see you all again,' he called then turned the horse towards James.

Emma put out her hand and waited as it approached before allowing her to gently touch its soft-as-velvet muzzle.

'I believe the time has come for us to go home. All will be well now. You'll see.'

The horse whinnied, calling to the others of its kind who were almost lost to sight.

'Come, James,' said Mr Witty, leaning down to help him onto the glowing steed. 'You too, Emma.'

'And me,' called Thomas. 'Don't forget me.'

'As if I would,' said the wizard, grinning as the cat jumped up between them and James began to laugh.

REUNION

At first, James couldn't make out where he was. Emma was sitting next to him, watching him anxiously. Daisy was stroking a big, black cat who was lying across the bottom of the bed.

'We didn't think you was going to wake up,' she said.

'Yes,' said Emma. 'We were beginning to think you were going to sleep forever.'

James looked around him, realising he really was at home.

'We did it then.'

Emma nodded.

Daisy pulled at the bedclothes. 'Get up,' she said. 'Daddy's home.'

As she spoke, his father's head poked around the door.

'Ah.' he said. 'Good. Glad to see you've had a good rest. Well done.'

Emma walked towards the door, taking Daisy with her.

'See you later, James. Oh. Auntie Caroline's asked me if I'd like to go and live with her.'

'And?' asked James.

She hesitated before answering.

'Not sure. Said I'd think about it.'

'What's there to think about?'

'Nothing, really.' She turned with a big grin on her face. ''spect I will then.'

'Good idea,' said his father as she left. 'Nice girl.'

'Yeah. She's all right.' James knew she could still hear him.

He found his mother in the kitchen with Daisy. She was chuckling to herself as she hurried towards him, giving him a great, big hug.

'What's the joke?'

129

'Oh. Just Daisy, who now tells me she can talk to mice. Two of them, in fact. Must be lovely to have such a vivid imagination.'

Auntie Cei did her best not to show her amusement as James said, 'Good job we've got that cat then, or is he going to live with you instead?'

'Maybe,' his aunt replied. 'But you can never tell with cats. No doubt he'll decide which suits him best.'

'You off then?'

'Almost ready,' she said. 'Just a few loose ends to attend to. Must make sure I don't leave anything important behind.'

As she spoke, James glimpsed a bright flash of blue as Kob peeped out from behind her. He nodded briefly and a silver whistle materialised into James's hand. Auntie Cei quickly shooed him through the kitchen door.

'Coming now,' she called out to Mrs Fellows as she made her way towards the car, keeping Kob hidden in front of her.

James turned as his father came in to wave them goodbye. 'Will you be staying at home now, Dad?'

His father smiled.

'I hope so. Still got quite a way to go, I think. But I'm much better now. I'm not quite sure what happened, James. I kept having a very disturbing dream that you were in some kind of trouble. I remember calling out to you. You seemed to be running away from something awful. When I finally woke up, I just knew I had to get better. Somehow the dream seemed so real it made me think I was losing you. Anyway, that was the turning point. Thinking about you helped me, and so here I am.'

They watched as the car moved slowly down the drive. The whistle was warm in James's hand. As his aunt approached the woods, a large, brown owl swooped towards them, trailing what looked like multicoloured party bubbles in its wake.

Then, as his father left the kitchen, James sighed and looked across at the cat, who sat up and winked at him.

Lightning Source UK Ltd.
Milton Keynes UK
UKOW02f0656201016

285716UK00001B/56/P